"You Only Used Me For Sex!" Nick Raged.

Tabitha gasped as she realized that his deep voice was carrying in the outside air, and that her grinning neighbors had heard and were having a field day. She blushed furiously.

Nick looked around at the neighborhood audience, cold mockery in the smile that flared on his handsome face. "Ruined your spotless reputation, have I?" he asked her. "Well, that's what you get for seducing innocent men and then dropping them when someone else comes along!"

"Damn you, Nick!" she yelled. "I wouldn't marry you if you had buckets of money and covered me in precious jewels!"

"I don't marry fickle women," he told her. "You two-timing Jezebel!"

"Look who's talking!" she shouted. "The playboy of the western world."

"At least I was reformed. You're just getting started!"

MOST WANTED:

Diana Palmer's exciting new series is coming your way. Whatever you want—they've got! Don't miss these compelling heroes, or these tantalizing romances—only from Silhouette Desire.

Dear Reader:

Believe it or not, it's been ten years since Silhouette Desire first made its way from us, the publisher, to you, the readers! And what a wonderful ten years it's been. Silhouette Desire stories are chock-full of delicious sensuality combined with deep emotions. Silhouette Desire is romance at its finest.

To celebrate this decade of delight, I'm proud to present our JUNE GROOMS, six stories about men and marriage. Each of these stories is unique: some are about men who marry—and some are about men whose main goal in life is to *avoid* wedded bliss! But all of these romances concern men who finally meet their match in one special woman.

The authors involved are some of the finest that Silhouette Desire has to offer: Ann Major, Naomi Horton, Raye Morgan, Suzanne Simms, Diana Palmer (with the next installment of her MOST WANTED series!) and Dixie Browning (with a terrific *Man of the Month!*). Some of these stories are serious; some are humorous—all are guaranteed to bring you hours of reading pleasure.

As an extra special treat, these six authors have written letters telling what they like about Silhouette Desire and discussing their feelings about romance . . . and marriage.

These books are our anniversary presents to you, our readers. I know you'll enjoy reading JUNE GROOMS as much as I did. And here's to the *next* ten years!

Sincerely,

Lucia Macro
Senior Editor

DIANA PALMER
THE CASE OF THE
CONFIRMED BACHELOR

SILHOUETTE *Desire*®

Published by Silhouette Books New York

America's Publisher of Contemporary Romance

To Diane, Sydney and my Roz

SILHOUETTE BOOKS
300 East 42nd St., New York, N.Y. 10017

THE CASE OF THE CONFIRMED BACHELOR

Copyright © 1992 by Diana Palmer

ISBN: 0-373-05715-6

First Silhouette Books printing June 1992

All the characters in this book have no existence outside the imagination of the author and have no relation whatsoever to anyone bearing the same name or names. They are not even distantly inspired by any individual known or unknown to the author, and all incidents are pure invention.

®: Trademark used under license and registered in the United States Patent and Trademark Office and in other countries.

Printed in the U.S.A.

Books by Diana Palmer

Silhouette Desire

The Cowboy and the Lady #12
September Morning #26
Friends and Lovers #50
Fire and Ice #80
Snow Kisses #102
Diamond Girl #110
The Rawhide Man #157
Lady Love #175
Cattleman's Choice #193
The Tender Stranger #230
Love by Proxy #252
Eye of the Tiger #271
Loveplay #289
Rawhide and Lace #306
Rage of Passion #325
Fit for a King #349
Betrayed by Love #391
Enamored #420
Reluctant Father #469
Hoodwinked #492
His Girl Friday #528
Hunter #606
Nelson's Brand #618
The Best Is Yet To Come #643
‡*The Case of the
  Mesmerizing Boss* #702
‡*The Case of the
  Confirmed Bachelor* #715

Silhouette Special Edition

Heather's Song #33
The Australian #239

Silhouette Romance

Darling Enemy #254
Roomful of Roses #301
Heart of Ice #314
Passion Flower #328
Soldier of Fortune #340
After the Music #406
Champagne Girl #436
Unlikely Lover #472
Woman Hater #532
*Calhoun #580
*Justin #592
*Tyler #604
*Sutton's Way #670
*Ethan #694
*Connal #741
*Harden #783
*Evan #819
*Donavan #843

Silhouette Books

Silhouette Christmas Stories 1987
''The Humbug Man''
Silhouette Summer Sizzlers 1990
''Miss Greenhorn''

Also by Diana Palmer

Diana Palmer Duets Books I-VI

*Long, Tall Texans
‡Most Wanted Series

Dear Readers,

It is my great pleasure to participate in the June Grooms special event at Silhouette Desire. I have been married for twenty years, very happily, and I believe that marriage is one of the most beautiful experiences in life.

I hope that all of you enjoy this special group of books as much as I have enjoyed writing my contribution to it. God bless each of you!

Love,

Diana Palmer

One

It was a lazy day in late spring. Nick Reed was feeling restless again. Working for Dane Lassiter's Houston detective agency had been exciting at first, and he'd enjoyed the work. But wanderlust called to him through the open window from the park across the way.

He watched a particularly trim young woman strolling along with a small furry dog and he smiled, because her pert figure reminded him of Tabby.

Tabitha Harvey. Shades of the past, he mused, leaning back in his chair. He'd deliberately avoided thinking about her over the past few months, because of what had happened when he and his sister, Helen, had flown back to their childhood home in Washington, D.C., on business. The trip had been right before New Year's, and Tabby had been around. That was natural, because she and Helen had been friends forever. They'd all been invited to a party together.

Nick had noticed that Tabby was watching him with unusual interest that night. She'd gone back to the punch bowl several times, as he had himself. But the punch had been spiked and Tabby hadn't known. She'd cornered Nick in a deserted room and started kissing him.

He could still feel her fervent, if untutored, mouth trembling under his lips. For a few seconds, he'd returned her kisses with everything in him. But he'd stopped her then, and demanded an explanation.

Fuzzily she'd explained that she knew he'd come all that way just to see her, that she knew he was finally ready to settle down. They'd be so happy, she said dreamily, smiling through an alcoholic haze.

Nick had no idea where she'd come up with those wild statements. If he'd ever thought of Tabby romantically, it had been years ago. Her remarks had come right out of the blue, and he'd reacted with shocked anger. He'd said some cutting and sarcastic things about her confession, which had sent her running. He'd gone back to the house with Helen and packed to leave D.C. He'd never told Helen exactly what happened, but he imagined Tabby had. He and Tabby hadn't had any contact since. Not that he wasn't sorry for the things he'd said; apologies were just hard for him.

He was scowling over the memories when Helen tapped at his office door and let herself in.

"Have you thought it over?" she asked eagerly.

He glowered at her, swinging his chair back around with a long, powerful leg. His blond hair gleamed like gold in the light from the window. His eyes, as dark as her own, had a hard glitter.

"Yes."

"You'll do it?" she asked with a grin, pushing her long hair back from her elfin face.

"Yes, I've thought about it, and no, I won't do it," he clarified.

Her face fell. "Nick! Please!"

"I won't," Nick said firmly. "You'll have to get your information some other way."

"Blood is thicker than water, remember," Helen Reed persisted hopefully. "I'm the only sister you have. There's only the two of us. Oh, Nick, you've got to!"

"Not really," he said with maddening indifference and a grin.

There were times, she thought, when he'd look really good hanging from a long rope. But then she'd be alone in the world except for Harold, to whom she was engaged.

"You're the only ex-FBI agent we've got at the Lassiter Detective Agency," she reminded him. "You've got contacts in all the right places. All you have to do is make one little-bitty telephone call," she persisted.

And she fixed her big brown eyes on him in their thin elfin face in its frame of long, straight brown hair. Except for his blond hair, they looked very much alike. Same stubborn chin, same elegant nose, same spirited dark eyes. But Nick was much more intro-verted and secretive than she was. He'd been that way all their lives, since they'd grown up in Washington, D.C.—where she attended college and he worked for the FBI.

Over the years, he'd done a lot of traveling, and she hadn't seen him for months, sometimes years at a time, until he'd received the offer of work from Richard Dane Lassiter. He'd met Dane on a case just before the Texas Ranger had been shot to pieces. When Lassiter began his own private detective agency, he coaxed Nick away from the FBI and Nick volunteered Helen as a paralegal, with her two years of business college giving her an edge over the competition. She'd come hotfoot from Washington to be with her brother. Their parents had been dead for some time, and she'd liked the idea of being near the last of her kin.

She did miss Tabitha Harvey very much at first, because she and Tabby had been friends since they were children. They still corresponded, although Tabby was very careful not to ask how Nick was. Obviously her memories of Helen's brother were painful ones.

"No," he said again. "I won't call the FBI for you."

She grinned at him, her slender hands together. "I'll tell."

"You'll tell what?"

"That you were out with that gorgeous blonde when you were supposed to be on stakeout for Dane," she said.

"Go ahead and tell him. She was my contact. I don't play around on the job."

"You do play around, though," Helen said, suddenly serious. "You never take women seriously."

He shrugged. "I don't dare. I'm not made for a pipe and slippers and kids. I like traveling and dangerous work, and the occasional pretty blonde when I'm *not* on stakeout."

"Pity," she sighed, smiling up at him. "You'd look nice covered in confetti."

"Who'd have me?" He grinned.

She had to bite her tongue to keep from mentioning Tabby's name. She'd done that once, and he'd gone right through the ceiling. He hadn't seen Tabby since New Year's Eve, when he'd gone with Helen to see about their parents' house in a small Washington suburb called Torrington. Tabby's father had died two years before, but she was still living in his house. It was next door to the Reeds. Nick had never discussed what happened when he and Tabby had talked one night while they were in Torrington, but it had caused him to bristle at the mention of her name ever since.

"The renters have moved out of Dad's house, you know," she said suddenly. "I can't fly back there and take care of it this time. Can you?"

His face hardened. "Why can't you?"

"Because I'm engaged, Nick," she said, exasperated. "You aren't. You're due for a vacation anyway, aren't you? You could kill two birds with one stone."

"I suppose I could," he said reluctantly, and his eyes darkened for an instant. Then he looked over his sister's head and his brows shot up. "Here comes the boss. Better vanish, before you become another statistic on the unemployment rolls."

"I wish you were on a roll. Filleted!" She chuckled.

He sauntered off, leaving her to Dane.

"Problems?" Dane asked, his eyes going from Nick back to Helen.

"Not a single one, boss," she assured him. "Nick and I were only discussing food."

"Okay. How about the Smart investigation?"

She grimaced. "I need one piece of information I can't dig out," she said miserably. "I can't get anybody to talk to me about Kerry Smart's brief stint with the FBI."

"Didn't you ask your brother? He has contacts over at the FBI office."

"That's why I'd like him filleted on a roll," she said sweetly. "He won't call anybody."

"Well, I can't order him to," he reminded her. "Nick's very secretive about his FBI days. He never talks about that period of his life. Perhaps he doesn't want any contact with the agency."

"I guess. Well, I'll trudge over to see Adams. He used to have one or two confidants."

"Good."

"How's our Tess, and the baby?"

"She's great, and the baby never sleeps. The doctor says he will one day," he added wistfully. "Meanwhile, it's just one more thing we can do together—sitting up with baby."

"You know you love it," she reminded him.

"Indeed I do. I could live without breathing much easier than I could live without my family."

"And there you were, a confirmed bachelor." She shook her head. "How are the mighty fallen!"

"Watch it," he threatened, "before you become redundant."

"Not me, boss. I intend to be even more valuable than Nick, if you'll just give me a few days off to work for the FBI so that I HAVE SOME CONTACTS I CAN USE WHEN I NEED THEM!" she said loudly, so that Nick heard her. But it didn't work. He made her a mocking bow and went out the door.

"One day, he'll deck you, Reed," Dane mused. "Sister or not, he's all for woman's lib. Equal opportunity, even in brawls, was how he put it."

"That's how I trained him," she said, tongue-in-cheek, and got a laugh for her pains.

"I'll tell him you said so."

"God forbid!" she said with a mock shudder. "You can't imagine what he told Harold the other day about what I did when I was two."

"You'll have to make sure he and Harold don't meet too often."

"That's what Harold says!" she confided mischievously.

She got her things together and wished she had the time to go and see Tess and the baby. But now that Tess had married Dane and they had a child of their own, it had put some distance between the two women. They still had lunch together occasionally, but Tess was closer to her friend Kit than she was to Helen.

Helen went to see Adams, who actually did have a contact in the FBI office. He made one telephone call and got her the information she needed.

"Quick work! Thanks!" she said enthusiastically.

He cleared his throat. "If Harold isn't treating you to pizza I'll buy you a beer," Adams offered. "Just casual, you know. I know you're engaged."

She smiled. He was nice. Big and burly and a little potbellied, but nice. "Thanks, Adams," she said sincerely. "Rain check?"

"Sure," he said easily. He grinned and went out the door. He always seemed to be by himself. Helen felt a bit sorry for him, but he was the kind of man who got attached to people and couldn't let go. She was afraid of that kind of involvement. Well, with anyone except Harold.

"So, what did you talk to Adams about?" Nick asked from behind her as she went out the door.

She gasped and then laughed. "I didn't hear you!"

"Of course you didn't," he said pleasantly. "I'm a private detective. We're trained to sneak up on people without being noticed."

"Really?" she asked, smiling. "I didn't know that."

He glared at her. "Nice to know you love me. What were you doing over there," he gestured toward Adams's now-deserted desk. "Warding off Adams?"

"No! I like Adams."

"Sure. I do, too, but he's a tick. If you ever get him attached to you, you'll have to stick a lighted match to his head to make him let go."

She burst out laughing. "You animal!" she gasped.

"You know I'm right. He's not a bad dude, all the same."

"Neither are you, once in a while."

"Get what you needed?"

She nodded. "No thanks to you," she said.

He shrugged indifferently. "It's no bad thing to teach you to be self-sufficient. I won't always be around."

The way he said that worried her. "Nick..." she began.

"I'm not dying of something," he said when he saw her expression, and he smiled. "I mean I'm getting restless. I may be moving on sometime soon."

"Wanderlust again?" she asked gently.

He nodded. "I get bored in the same place."

"Go home," she said. "Take a vacation. Relax."

"In Washington?" His eyes widened. "Funny girl!"

"You'll find a way. It's a quiet street. No drug dealers, no shoot-outs. Just peace and quiet."

"And your friend Tabby right next door," he said icily.

"Tabby's dating a very nice historian at her college," she told him, enjoying the way his eyelids flickered. "I think it may be serious. So you won't have to hide from her while you're there."

"She wasn't dating anybody when we were there earlier in the year," he said. He sounded as if he thought she'd betrayed him.

"That was then," she reminded him. "A lot can happen in a few months. Tabby's twenty-five. It's time she married and had kids. She's settled and has a good job."

He didn't answer her. He looked hunted. He *felt* hunted. So he changed the subject without appearing to be evasive. "Did you get your information from Adams?" he asked her again.

"Yes. I had to have it to finish my case," she said. "Dane was just asking me how far I'd gotten earlier. The client needs the background information. He hopes it may help him avert a court case."

"I see." His fingers traced a teasing line down her nose. "I don't suppose it occurred to you that I might have a damned good reason for not wanting to talk to people I used to know at the agency?"

Her dark eyes searched his curiously. Her handsome brother had bone structure an artist would love—from his high cheekbones to his straight nose and perfectly chiseled masculine mouth.

"You're staring. And you haven't answered me," he said.

"I was just thinking what a dish you are," she said with a grin. "You look just like Dad. No wonder women threaten to leap off buildings when you throw them over. You never talk about the time you spent with the FBI, and I never knew why. I thought maybe you missed it."

"Sometimes I do," he confessed. "Not often. But it's never a good idea to open up old wounds. Sometimes they bleed."

"Yes," she said absently, "I suppose so."

"All right. Have a sandwich with me and we'll talk about what we're going to do with the house. I'm tired of renting it out. Too much hassle. I want to talk to you about selling it."

"Sell our legacy?" she burst out.

He sighed. "I figured you'd react that way. Come on. Let's eat. We can fight over dessert."

He took her to a nice seafood restaurant. She'd been expecting a hamburger, and she paused self-consciously at the door, nervous in her old black skirt and black-and-white checked blouse, her hair loose and unkempt.

"Now what's the matter?" he asked impatiently.

"Nick, I'm not dressed for a place like this," she said earnestly. "Can't we go someplace less expensive?"

"I beg your pardon?"

"A fast-food place," she explained. "Plastic cartons? Paper sacks? Foam cups?"

"Nonbiodegradable litter." He frowned. "No way. Come on." He took her arm and forcibly led her inside. He chuckled as he seated her, very elegantly, at a table. "I hope you aren't really that mad for pizza. They don't serve it here."

She smiled. "Harold and I are sort of tired of it, if you want the truth," she confessed as he sat down across from her. The table had a burning red candle in a glass chimney. The lighting was cozy, like the atmosphere with its classical music playing unobtrusively overhead.

"I like service," he said. "Old-fashioned service, and good food. They have both here."

Even as he spoke, a slender blonde paused beside the table and presented them with menus. Her eyes lingered on Nick's face while he ordered coffee, to give them time to decide on a choice of entrée.

"Thanks, Jean," he said warmly.

The woman smiled back and with an envious glance at Helen, went on her way.

"She likes you," she said.

"I know. I like her, too. But that's all it is," he added, his face very serious as he met Helen's curious stare. "Stop trying to play matchmaker. You only complicate lives."

He sounded incredibly bitter. "Are you trying to tell me something?" she asked quietly.

"You threw me together with Tabby at that New Year's Eve party the last time we were home. You didn't mention that you'd told her I flew all the way from Houston just to take her out."

He hadn't talked about this before. She felt guilty and apprehensive at his tone. "I didn't think it would hurt," she began.

He cut her off. "She had some crazy idea that my feelings had changed and I wanted a relationship with her," he said curtly, his eyes accusing. "I wasn't expecting it and I overreacted. She cried." His face went harder. "In all the years we've known Tabby, I've never seen her cry. It really got to me."

Helen knew Nick well enough to guess what happened next. "You lost your temper," she guessed.

"I told you, I wasn't expecting it. One minute she was telling me about some new find they were studying in the anthropology department, the next she was off on a tangent about the future."

"The punch was spiked," she said. "I didn't know. I poured her two cups of it."

"I finally figured out for myself that she was three sheets to the wind, but that sudden burst of affection knocked me off balance," he replied. He rammed his hands into his pockets and looked uncomfortable. "I panicked. Tabby's a sweet woman, but she's not my type."

"Who is?" she challenged. "You make confirmed bachelors look like old married men. You could do a lot worse than Tabby."

"She could do a lot better than me," he countered. "A little cottage with a picket fence isn't what I'm saving up for. I want to sail around the world. I want to go exploring. In the meantime, I like being an investigator, even if this job is beginning to wear on me."

"Tabby's an investigator, did you know? She searched for the solutions to ancient mysteries. That's what anthropologists do—they discover the cultures of ancient civilizations and how they worked."

"No two-thousand-year-old mummy is likely to sit up in his sarcophagus and pull a gun on her, either," he argued.

"Probably not," she conceded. "But digging for the truth is something you both like to do."

He ran an angry hand around the back of his neck. "I didn't like hurting her that way," he said abruptly. "I said some harsh things."

"Well, that's all in the past now," she reminded him. "She's dating someone and it sounds serious, so you won't have to worry about any complications while you're deciding what we should do about Dad's house."

"I suppose not," he said, but he wasn't looking forward to seeing Tabby again. His treatment of her wore on his nerves, and she wasn't going to be pleased to see him. Tabby, like Nick himself, deplored losing control. Her lack of pride was going to hurt her as much as Nick's sharp words, and she wouldn't like being reminded of their confrontation any more than he did.

"It will be all right," Helen said gently.

"Your favorite saying. What if it isn't?"

"For goodness' sake, think positively!" she chided. "Buy a plane ticket and go to Washington."

"I guess I will. But I still have my doubts," he said.

Two days later, with Dane Lassiter's blessing, Nick was on his way down Oak Lane to his father's old house in Torrington.

It looked just the same, he thought as he wheeled lazily along in the rental car. The oaks were a little older, as he was, but the street was quiet and dignified, like the mostly elderly people who lived on it.

His eyes went involuntarily over the flat front of the redbrick home where he and Helen had grown up. There were blooming shrubs all around it and the dogwood and cherry trees were green now with their blossoms gone in late spring. The weather was comfortably warm without being blazing hot, and everything looked green and restful. He hadn't realized before just how tired he was. This vacation was probably a good idea after all, even if he had fought like a tiger to keep from taking it.

It was Friday, and not quitting time, so he didn't expect to see Tabby at her family's house next door. But in his mind's eye, he saw her—long brown hair down to her waist and big dark eyes that followed him everywhere as she walked by the house on her way home from school. She was tall, very slender, with curves that weren't noticeable at all. That hadn't changed. Her hair was in a bun these days, not long and windblown. She wore little makeup and clothes that were stylish but not sexy. Her body was as slender as it had been in her teens, nothing to make any man particularly amorous unless he loved her. Poor Tabby. He felt sorry for her, angry at Helen because she'd engineered that meeting at New Year's Eve and made Tabby think he cared about her.

He did, in a sort of brotherly way, mainly because that was how he'd always interpreted Tabby's attitude toward him. She'd never seemed to want a physical relationship with him. Not until New Year's Eve, anyway, and she had been intoxicated. Perhaps this colleague she was dating did love her, and would make her happy. He hoped so.

Life in a garret wasn't for him. He was already thinking about applying to Interpol or as a customs inspector down in the Caribbean. A tame existence appealed to him about as much as drowning.

He pulled into the driveway of his father's house and sat just looking at it quietly for a long time. Home. He hadn't ever thought about what it meant to have a place to come back to. Odd, with his need for freedom, that it felt so wonderful to be in his own driveway. Possession was new to him, like the feeling of emptiness he'd had since the Christmas holidays. Loneliness wasn't something he'd experienced before. He wondered why he should feel that way, as if he were missing out on life, when his life was so full and exciting.

As he unlocked the front door and carried his suitcase inside, he drank in the smells of wood and varnish and freshener, because he'd had a woman come in and clean every week since the house had been vacant. His parents' things were neatly kept, just as they'd been when he and Helen were children. Nothing changed here. The smells and sights were those of his boyhood. Familiar things, that gave him a sense of security.

He scowled, looking toward the banister of the staircase that led up to the three bedrooms on the second floor. His long fingers touched the antique wood and fondled it absently. Selling the furnished house had seemed the thing to do. Now, he wasn't sure about it.

As the day wore on, he became less sure. The power had been turned on earlier in the week, and the refrigerator and stove were in good working order. He found a coffeemaker stashed under the sink. He went shopping for supplies, arriving home just as a small blue car pulled in next door.

He paused on the steps, two grocery bags in one powerful arm, watching as a woman stepped out of the car. She didn't look toward him, not once. Her carriage very correct, almost regal, she walked to the front door of her house, inserted the key she held ready in her hand, and disappeared out of sight.

Tabby. He stared after her without moving for a minute. She hadn't changed. He hadn't expected her to. But it felt different to look at her now, and it puzzled him. He couldn't quite determine what the difference was.

He went inside and started a pot of coffee before he fried a steak and made a salad for his supper. While he was eating it, he pondered on Tabby's lack of interest in his presence. She had to have seen the car in the driveway, seen him go to the door. But she hadn't looked his way, hadn't spoken.

He felt depressed suddenly, and regretted even more the wall he'd built between them at New Year's. They were old friends. Almost family. It would have been nice to sit down with Tabby and talk about the old days when they'd all played together as children. He didn't suppose Tabby would want to talk to him now.

After he'd finished his meal and washed up the dishes, he sat down in the living room with a detective novel. The television wasn't working. He didn't really mind. It was like entertainment overkill these days, with channels that never shut down and dozens of programs to choose from. The constant bombardment sometimes got on his nerves, so he shut it off and read instead. Nothing like a good book, he thought, to cultivate what Agatha Christie's hero Hercule Poirot called the "little gray cells."

He was knee-deep in the mystery novel when the front door knocker sounded.

Curious, he went to open the door.

Tabby stood there, unsmiling, her hair in a neat bun, her glasses low on her nose, her expression one of strain and worry. She was wearing a neat suit with a white blouse, and she obviously had worn it all day. It was nine in the evening and she hadn't changed into casual clothes.

"Hello," he said. His heart felt lighter and he smiled.

Tabby didn't return the smile. Her hands were folded very tightly at her waist. "I wouldn't have bothered you," she said stiffly, "but I don't really know any other detectives. It seemed almost providential that you came home today."

"Did it? Why?" he asked.

She swallowed. "I'm under suspicion of theft," she said. Her lower lip trembled, but only for an instant until she got it under control. Her head lifted even higher with stung pride. "I haven't taken anything, and I haven't been formally charged, but only I had access to the artifact that's disappeared. It's a small vase with cuneiform writing that dates to the Sumerian empire, and they think I stole it."

Two

Nick's dark blond eyebrows rose curiously. "You, a thief? My God, you walked two blocks to return a dollar old man Forbes lost when you were just sixteen. People don't change that much in nine years."

She seemed to relax. "Thanks for the vote of confidence, but I need proof that I didn't do it. If you're going to be in town for a few days, I want to employ you to clear me."

"Employ for pete's sake!" he growled. "Honest to God, Tabby, you don't have to hire me to do you a favor!"

"It's business," she said firmly. "And I'm not a pauper. I don't need to impose on our old friendship."

"You can't imagine how prissy you sound," he mused, his dark eyes twinkling as they searched hers. "Come in here and talk to me about it."

"I, uh, I can't do that," she said, glancing uneasily around her as if there were eyes behind every curtain.

"Why not?"

"It's quite late, and you're alone in the house," she reminded him.

He gaped at her. "Are you for real?" He scowled and leaned closer, making a sniffing sound. "Tipsy, are we?" he asked with a wicked gleam in his eyes.

"I am not!" she said stiffly, flushing. "And I wish you'd forget that. I was drunk!"

"Absolutely," he agreed. "I've never seen you with a snootful. Your mask slipped."

"It won't ever slip again like that," she told him. "I hope I didn't embarrass you."

"Not really. Why can't you come inside? I almost never have sex with women in suits."

The color in her cheeks got worse. "Now cut that out!"

He shrugged. "If you say so." He folded his arms across his broad chest. His shirt was unfastened at the collar, where a thick golden thatch was just visible. It seemed to disturb Tabby, because her eyes quickly averted from it.

"I thought, if you had time, we might meet for lunch tomorrow and I'll fill you in."

He sighed with mock resignation. "There's not really any need for that." He reached beside him and turned the porch light on. Then he escorted her down the steps and neatly seated her on the middle step, lowering himself beside her. "Here we are, in the light, so that everyone in the neighborhood can see that we aren't naked. Is that better?"

"*Nick!*" she raged.

"Don't be so stuffy," he murmured. "You're living in the dark ages."

"A few of us need to or civilization as we know it may cease to exist," she returned hotly. "Haven't you noticed how things are going in our social structure?"

"Who hasn't?"

"Drugs, killer sexual diseases, streets full of homeless people, serial killers." She shook her head. "Anything goes may sound great, but it brings down civilizations."

"Most people don't know about ancient Rome," he reminded her. "You might start wearing a toga to get their attention."

She glowered at him. "You never change."

"Sure I do. I'd smell terrible wearing the same clothes over and over again."

She threw up her hands. It was just like old times, with Nick cracking jokes while her heart broke in two. Except that now it wasn't just her heart, it was her integrity and perhaps her professional future.

He touched her chin and turned her to face his eyes. The mockery was gone out of them as he asked, "Tell me about it, Tabby."

She drew back from the touch of his hands, so disturbing to her peace of mind. "There was an old piece of Sumerian pottery that I was using to show my students while I lectured on the Sumerian Empire. It was a very unique piece with cuneiform writing on it."

"You've lost me. It's been years since I took Western Civilization in college."

"Cuneiform was an improvement in the Sumerian culture, one step above pictographic writing," she explained. "In cuneiform, each wedge-shaped sign stands for a syllable. There are thousands of pieces of Sumerian writings contained on baked clay tablets. But this writing," she continued, "wasn't on a tablet, it was on a small vase, perfectly preserved and over five thousand years old." She leaned forward. "Nick, the college paid a small fortune for it. It was the most perfect little find I've ever seen, rare and utterly irreplaceable. I was allowed to use it for a visual aid in that one class. None of us dreamed that it would be lost. It cost thousands of dollars...!"

"Only the one artifact?"

"Yes," she agreed. "It was on my desk. I had to tutor a student in the classroom and I was going to put it back under lock and key afterward. I wasn't gone more than five minutes, but when I came back, it was missing. There was no one around, and I can't prove that I didn't take it."

"Can't the student vouch for you?"

"Of course, but not about the artifact. She never saw it."

He whistled. "No witnesses?"

She shook her head. "Not a one."

"Anyone with a motive for stealing it?"

"A find like that would be worth a fortune, but only to a collector," she admitted. "Most students simply see it as a minor curiosity. Only a few members of the faculty knew its actual value. Daniel, for one."

"Daniel?"

"He's a colleague of mine. Daniel Myers. We...go out together. He's honest," she added quickly. "He has too much integrity to steal anything."

"Most people who steal have integrity," he said cynically, "but their greed overrides it."

"That's not fair, Nick," she protested. "You don't even know Daniel."

"I guess not," he said, angered by her defense of the man. Who was this colleague, anyway? His dark eyes whipped down to catch hers. "Tell me about Daniel."

"He's very nice. Divorced, one son who's almost in his teens. He lives downtown in Washington and he's on staff at the college where I work."

"I didn't ask for his history. I said tell me about him."

"He's tall and slender and very intelligent."

"Does he love you?"

She shifted uncomfortably. "I don't think you need to know anything about my personal life. Only my professional one."

He sighed. "Well, you don't have anyone to look out for you," he reminded her. "I always used to when you were in your teens."

"That was then. I'm twenty-five now. I don't need looking after. Besides, you're only five years older than I am."

"Six, almost."

"Daniel wants to marry me."

"What do you get out of it if Daniel doesn't love you?"

"Will you take the case?" she asked, changing the subject abruptly.

"Of course. But Daniel had better not get in the way."

"Oh, he won't," she said, but with unvoiced reservations. Daniel tended to be just the least bit superior. He wouldn't like Nick, she decided. Worse, Nick already didn't like him. It was going to be a touchy situation, but she was sick with worry. She had to have someone in her corner, and who better than Nick, who was one of the best detectives in the world according to his sister Helen.

"I'd like to come around to the college tomorrow and get a look at where you work."

"Tomorrow is Saturday," she stammered.

"Classes won't be in session," he reminded her.

"Daniel was going to take me shopping..."

"Daniel can buy his clothes some other time."

"Not for clothes, for an engagement ring!"

His eyes narrowed. He hated *that* idea. Hated it, for reasons he couldn't put a finger on. "That will have to wait. I'm only going to be in town until next Friday."

"I'll phone him tonight."

"Good."

She got up, smoothing her skirt, and Nick rose with her, his face solemn, concerned. "Don't they know you at all, these colleagues?"

"Of course. But it does look bad. My office was locked at the time. Nobody else has a key."

Nails in her coffin, he was thinking, but he didn't say it. "Try not to worry. We'll muddle through."

"Okay. Thanks, Nick," she said without looking at him.

"No need for that. I'll call for you about eight in the morning. That too early?"

She shook her head. "I'm always up at dawn."

"Just like old times," he recalled. "I hope you don't have plans to climb the drain pipe, just like old times, and climb in a bedroom window."

She caught her breath. "It was only once or twice, and it was Helen's room I climbed into!"

"You were such a tomboy," he mused. "Hell with a bat in sandlot baseball, the most formidable tackle we had in football, and not a bad tree climber. You don't look much different today."

She grimaced. "Don't I know it." She sighed. "No matter what I eat, I can't put on a pound."

"Wait until you hit middle age."

"That's a few years away," she said with a faint smile.

"Yes. Quite a few. Get some sleep."

"You, too. Good night."

He returned the sentiment and watched her walk to her front door. Old times. He thought back to warm summer evenings when he'd bring his dates home and they'd all sit on chairs on the lawn and watch Helen and Tabby, who were a few years younger, chase fireflies on the lush lawn. He supposed Tabby would watch her own children do that very thing one day.

He didn't want to think about that. He went back inside and tried to pick up his mystery novel again, but he'd lost his taste for it. He put it down and went to bed, hours and hours before usual.

Tabby was dressed in a floral skirt and white knit blouse when he called for her the next morning just at eight. He wasn't much more dressed up than she was, comfortable in slacks and a red knit shirt. He scowled down at her.

"Must you always screw your hair up like that? I haven't seen it long in quite a while."

"It's hot around my neck," she said evasively. "I only let it down at night."

"For Daniel?" he asked sarcastically.

"Do we go in your car or mine?" she asked, ignoring the question.

"Mine, definitely," he said with a disparaging glance at hers. "I like having room for my head."

"The seat lets down."

"I can't drive lying on my back."

"Nick!"

"Come on." He led her to the big sedan he'd rented and helped her inside. "Direct me. It's been a long time since I've driven here."

"Not so long," she replied. "You didn't leave until you quit the FBI. That's only been about four years ago."

"It seems like forever sometimes."

"I guess Houston is a lot different."

"Only when it floods. Otherwise, it's a lot of concrete and steel and pavement. Just like every other city. It's Washington with a drawl."

She laughed softly. "I suppose most cities are alike. I haven't traveled much. And when I do, it's to places that seem pretty primitive by modern standards."

"To digs, I gather?"

"That's right. I went out to the Custer battlefield in Montana a few years ago to help archaeologists and other anthropologists identify some remains. Then I had a stint in Arizona with some Hohokam ruins and once I flew down to Georgia where they were excavating an eighteenth-century cabin."

"How exciting."

"Not to you," she conceded. "But it's life and breath to me. I want to investigate aboriginal sites in Australia and explore some of the Greek and Roman ruins they're just beginning to excavate. I want to go to Machu Pichu in Peru and to the Maya and Toltec

and Olmec ruins in Mexico and Central America."
Her eyes sparkled with excitement. "I want to go to
Africa and to China . . . Oh, Nick, there's a world of
mysteries out there just waiting to be solved!"

He glanced at her. "You sound like a detective."

"I am, sort of," she argued. "I look for clues in the
past, and you look for them in the present. It's still all
investigation, you know."

He turned his attention back to the road. "I suppose. It depends on your point of view."

She studied him briefly. "You aren't smoking. Hel-
en said you'd quit."

"Five weeks, now," he replied. "I only had the jit-
ters once Lassiter asked us all to give it up, to help him.
Tess made him quit," he said with a grin. "Imagine,
old Nail Eater being led around by a woman."

"I doubt she's leading him around. He probably
loves her and wants to make her happy. He'll live
longer if he doesn't smoke."

"We're all going to die eventually," he reminded
her. "Some of us might do it a little quicker, but we
don't have much choice."

"The law of entropy."

He cocked an eyebrow. "I beg your pardon?"

"That's what scientists call it—the law of entropy.
It means that everything grows old and dies."

"As long as we're scientific about it," he said
mockingly.

She adjusted her glasses, pushing them back up on
her nose. "No need to be sarcastic. Turn here." She
pointed.

He drove into the parking lot and pulled into a space
marked Visitors. "Why here?"

"You don't have a sticker that permits you to park here," she reminded him. "If you park in a student's spot, you'll be towed. I know you wouldn't like that."

"It's not my car," he reminded her.

"You rented it. You'd have to liberate it."

"I love the way you use words," he chuckled as he got out of the car and helped her out.

"Nice manners," she said, tongue-in-cheek.

"You opened the door for me back when I broke my leg in your senior year of school. Drove me back and forth to work every day, too, on your way."

"Wasn't I sweet?" she asked wistfully. "Ah, those good old days."

"You were less irritating then."

"So were you," she tossed back. She cocked her head and studied him. "Footloose Nick," she murmured. "I suppose you'll end up in a shoot-out with spies somewhere and they'll mount you on a wall or something."

He grinned. "Lovely thought. How kind of you."

She gave up. "My office is on the second floor."

She led him into the big brick building, past the admissions office and up the staircase that led to the history and sociology departments.

"I'm down the hall. The historians have this wing. The sociology department here is rather small, although we offer some interesting courses."

"Anthropology is sociology," he remarked. "I took one course of it in college myself. Sociology and law go hand in hand, did you know?"

"Sure!" she said, unlocking her office. "That's the biology lab down the hall. They're only up here temporarily while their facilities are being remodeled. They have snakes in there," she said with a shiver.

A primal scream echoed down the hall with its high ceilings. "Is that one of them?" he asked.

"Snakes don't scream," she muttered. "No, that's Pal."

"Who? Or should I say what?"

"Pal's a what, all right. He's the missing link. That's what we call him up here. Australopithecus insidious."

"Greek."

"Latin," she corrected. "Pidgin Latin. What I mean, is that Pal is too smart to be a monkey. We have to lock him up. He likes to rip up textbooks. And if you ever leave your keys lying around when he's on the loose, you'll never see them again."

"Isn't he caged?"

"Usually. He picks the lock." She laughed. "The last time he got out, the administrator and several members of the board of trustees were having a catered meeting in the conference room. Pal got in there and started pelting everybody with melon balls and rolls."

"I'll bet that went over well with the guests."

"Guest," she corrected. "It was a senator from Maryland. We never did get that funding we needed for a new research project."

"Why doesn't that surprise me? Out of idle curiosity, what were you going to research?"

Her eyes brightened. "Primate social behavior."

He burst out laughing. "It seems to me that you're doing enough of that without funding."

"That's exactly what our president said. Here." She opened the door to a Spartan office with a desk, a chair, and a bookcase jammed full of reference books. On her desk were stacks of paper and a college handbook. "Like most everyone else here, I'm a faculty advisor. In my spare time, I teach anthropology."

He stood looking down at her with open curiosity. "You were always a brain. I used to feel threatened by you sometimes. No matter what I knew, you seemed to know more."

"Brains can be a curse when you're a young girl," she replied with faint bitterness. "But they last a lot longer than a voluptuous figure and a pretty face," she added.

"There's nothing wrong with you," he mused. "Except that you need feeding up."

"Oh, I'll spread out one day. This is where the artifact was lying when it vanished."

She pointed to a central spot on the desk.

"How long ago did it walk off?"

"Yesterday afternoon."

He nodded and pulled a small leather-bound kit out of his pocket. "Go and read a book or make a telephone call for a few minutes while I do a little investigating."

"What are you going to do?"

"Dust your desk for fingerprints and look for clues, of course. Has anyone been at this desk except you since the artifact was taken?"

She shook her head.

"Good. That narrows it down a bit."

She started to ask him more questions, but he was knee-deep in thought and investigation. She shrugged and left him there.

Minutes later, he straightened, irritated by the lack of fingerprints. The desk had a rough surface, which made it hard to find a full print. But a tiny piece of what looked like hair lay on a white sheet of paper, and that he took with him, securing it with a pair of tweezers and sticking it in a tiny plastic bag that he then sealed. It wasn't much, but if it was human hair, the lab over at the FBI could tell them plenty about it. It was amazing how much data one strand of hair could provide. It was strangely coarse. He dismissed it instantly when Tabby came in the door, his eyes watchful as they skimmed over her. She made him feel as if he'd only just come back from a long journey. It was a very pleasant sensation. When he was with her, his restlessness seemed to go momentarily into eclipse.

"Anything?" Tabby asked hopefully.

Her question diverted him. "Not much," he said. "I couldn't get a full print...."

He stopped as a tall, unsmiling man appeared in the doorway behind Tabby.

"This is Dr. Daniel Myers," she introduced the newcomer, who was wearing a dark blue suit with a white shirt and conventional tie. On a Saturday, he was dressed like a preacher, which gave Nick a pretty accurate picture of his meticulous personality.

"Nick Reed," Nick said, introducing himself. He didn't offer his hand. Nor did Daniel, he noticed with some amusement.

"You must be discreet," he cautioned Nick. "I'm sure you understand what a theft like this could do to the image of Thorn College."

"Certainly," he agreed. "As aware as I am of what it could do to Tabby's future."

"Tabby?"

"Her family and mine have been close all our lives," Nick told the man.

"It sounds like something one would call a cat, don't you think, darling?" he asked Tabby, and slid a long arm over her thin shoulders.

Nick just stopped himself from leaping forward. Incredible, he thought, how his mind reacted to the sight. Tabby was like a sister to him. Perhaps he only felt protective. That had to be it.

He pocketed the sealed plastic envelope. "I'll run this over to the lab. I have a friend there."

"Will he be at work on Saturday?"

"Since I phoned him at home last night and asked him to meet me there, I do hope so," he replied.

"That was kind of him," she said.

"I'll drop you off on my way to FBI headquarters," he offered.

Daniel seemed to grow two feet. "That's hardly necessary," he said stiffly, and his arm drew Tabby closer. "Tabitha must have told you that we're to shop for an engagement ring today."

"Yes, I hear you're planning to be married," Nick said.

"A very sensible move, too," Daniel said carelessly. "I live alone and so does Tabitha. She had that huge house and lot, where we can live, and her car is paid for." He hugged her close. "She likes keeping house and cooking, so I'll have plenty of time to work on my book."

Nick was going to explode. He knew he was. "Book?"

"Our book," Tabby inserted with a glare at Daniel. "It's a new perspective on what I found at the Custer battlefield after the fire."

"And includes information I dug out about its history," Daniel added quickly. "Tabitha could hardly do it without my help on the grammar and punctuation."

Nick's eyebrows jerked up. "You think Tabby needs help with those? Are we talking about the girl who was school spelling champion in seventh grade and won a scholarship to Thorn College?"

Daniel shifted on his feet. "I have a master's degree in English." His watery blue eyes made mincemeat of Nick. "What was your field of study, Mr. Reed?" he asked with pleasant sarcasm, as if he considered that a detective probably had less than a high school education. In fact, an FBI agent was preferred to have a bachelor's degree in accounting or a law degree. Nick had a law degree. It wasn't something he'd ever boasted about. He wasn't going to now, either, if that careless, mocking smile he gave Daniel was any indication.

"Oh, I know a little about the law," Nick said. "I am, after all, a trained detective."

"Like a police officer." Daniel nodded, looking superior. "They're only required to have a high school education or its equivalent, I believe?"

Nick stiffened. But before he could explode, and he looked close to it, Tabby stepped in.

"We really have to go, Daniel," she said. "Thanks again, Nick. I'll talk to you later."

He murmured something and Tabby moved Daniel out into the hall with unusual dexterity.

"I don't like that man," Daniel said angrily as they walked down the hall.

"I know," she said, soothing him.

A loud screech sounded as they passed the temporary biology lab. "I don't like that monkey, either."

"Yes, Daniel. Let's go."

A door opened at the end of the hall and a small man with a moustache came out, pausing as he saw Daniel and Tabby. He looked uncomfortable for an instant. "Uh, the missing artifact," he said to Tabby. "Found it yet?"

"No. But I've engaged a private detective to look for it," she began.

Dr. Flannery stood very still for a moment. "Detective?"

"Just to look for the pottery," she said.

"Of course. Of course." He turned and moved off down the hall, stopped suddenly, turned and went back the other way with a mumbled goodbye.

"Flannery is a flake," Daniel muttered as they left the building. "He spends too much time with those monkeys. He's beginning to act like them."

"Primates," she corrected. "They're very nice when you get to know them. Even Pal. He's intelligent, you know, that's why he gets into so much trouble."

"Maybe Flannery took that piece of pottery," he said speculatively. "Did you know that his house was repossessed just recently? He's in financial trouble. Some collectors would pay anything for a find like that."

"Yes, I know. But it couldn't have been Dr. Flannery," she said stubbornly. "My goodness, he's a biologist, not a thief!"

"Desperate men do desperate things," he said. He slid his hand into hers. "You are going to marry me, aren't you? We're very compatible, and this will certainly be a successful book. Probably the first of many." His eyes had a faraway look. "I've always dreamed of being in print."

"Daniel, you aren't marrying me so that we can write a book together, are you?" she teased.

He cleared his throat. "Of course not. Don't be silly."

She wasn't being silly. Daniel kissed her only when he had to, and not very enthusiastically. He'd never tried to step over the line, to be amorous. He never sent her flowers or phoned her at midnight just to talk. He only ever talked about writing. She sighed. Marriage was what she'd always wanted, but this wasn't how she'd envisioned it. Not at all like this.

Her dreams had been passionate ones, full of Nick. Dreams died hard, and hers never had. Now that he was back in her life, she'd have to start all over again forgetting him. Perhaps, she thought, it would be easier when he left. Meanwhile, all she had to do was live through the next week, and hope that he could clear her name. If he couldn't, she thought with real fear, she might not even have a job much longer!

Tabitha couldn't find a ring she liked. Honestly, she wasn't that interested in marrying Daniel at all. He seemed bent on using her, while she was hitting back at Nick in the only way she knew. It was ridiculous to promise to marry one man just to show another that someone found her desirable. As if Nick was fooled! He'd seen right through Daniel's motives for the engagement. Probably through Tabby's, too. She flushed.

Daniel had taken her to a nice restaurant for lunch. She was nibbling dessert while he went to the bathroom.

Her mind was far away from the strawberry short-cake she was eating. It was on that fatal New Year's Eve party.

She'd felt as if anything was possible that night. She'd been wearing a black dress with spaghetti straps, her long hair around her shoulders. She'd left her glasses off—despite the fact that she was nearly blind without them—and put on much more makeup than usual. Helen had told her that Nick was finally ready to settle down and that it was Tabby he really wanted. That bit of encouragement had been just enough, along with the alcohol, to make her act totally out of character.

Nick, gloriously handsome Nick, had been leaning against a door frame sipping punch. Tabby had stared at him with her heart in her eyes, drowning in the sight of him. She'd loved him for, oh, so long!

Putting her punch on a nearby table, she'd walked a little unsteadily to where he was standing in the shadows of the room while sultry blues music played from the stereo nearby.

"All alone, Nick?" she'd asked, with pouting lips.

He'd smiled indulgently. "Not now," he mused. "You look nice, Tabby. Very grown-up."

"I'm twenty-five."

"That wasn't what I meant. You aren't very worldly."

"I'm working on it," she purred. "Want to see?"

She noted the faint surprise on his face as she suddenly stepped close to him, smoothing her slender body completely against his.

"Tabby!" he exclaimed.

"It's all right," she'd whispered nervously. "I only want to kiss you, Nick. And kiss you...and kiss you...!"

She'd reached up while she was speaking and looped her arms around his neck to draw his shocked face within reach. She knew little about men and less about kissing with her mostly academic background, but she loved him and she put her heart into it.

She seemed to shock him. His body froze for a few seconds. Then his dark eyes closed and his mouth hardened, and all at once, it was Nick who was doing the kissing. His steely arm clenched around her and jerked her into his body, one powerful leg moving just enough to let her slim figure intimately close while the kiss went on and on. His lips lifted while he breathed unsteadily.

"Is this what you want?" he asked roughly.

"Yes," she breathed, coaxing his mouth back to hers. "Do it again," she whispered against his hard lips.

He obliged her. The glass of punch found its way onto a table. They were hidden from the rest of the partygoers by a large potted plant and an alcove, but Tabby was beyond knowing where they were. She let her hands slide up and down his long back, gave her mouth to him totally even when he deepened the kiss far beyond her meager experience. She began to moan softly when she felt Nick's thighs against her.

That was when he jerked back and pushed her away with a vicious motion of his lean hands.

"What the hell are you doing?" he demanded harshly, his dark eyes blazing. "You're no drunken floozy out for a cheap roll in the hay, are you? Or is that what you do want?" he added with an insolent laugh. "Do you want me, Tabby? There's probably a room upstairs that we could use. Or as a last resort, we could go out on the patio into a dark corner and pull up your skirt..."

She'd cried out at his remarks. "No! Nick, I want to marry you," she'd blurted. "I know you're ready to settle down. I want to have children with you. Isn't that why you came back?"

His face had actually paled. "I came back to check on my father's house. Nothing more."

"But... But I thought..." She swallowed and went deathly pale. "I thought you wanted me."

"A dried-up spinster with a computer for a brain and no breasts to speak of?" he asked arrogantly. "My God, did you really?"

She ran. She turned and ran out the door and went straight home—blind and deaf to the turmoil she'd created in the face of the man she'd left behind. Helen had come after her and she'd cried on her friend's shoulder until dawn, only then swearing Helen to secrecy about her anguish.

She hadn't touched a drop of liquor since, and the shame lingered. But Nick would never know how badly he'd hurt her. All she required now was his help to clear her name. And then maybe she would—and maybe she wouldn't—actually marry Daniel.

Having Nick come back was slowly clearing away the desperation and madness of the past few empty months. She could see what she'd been doing, trying to substitute Daniel for the man she wanted. She couldn't have Nick, but she didn't need to make herself and Daniel miserable by trying to replace him with someone who would never be more than second best.

That decided, finally, she smiled at Daniel when he came back and managed to keep the conversation on just a friendly level for the rest of the afternoon.

Three

Nick had always been fascinated by the forensics lab at FBI headquarters. It had a reputation second to none for being able to put together evidence from almost nothing. A human hair with its DNA structure could yield a pattern as individual as a fingerprint. The tread of a tennis shoe involved in a murder could be traced to the person who purchased it. A scrap of cloth could yield an incredible amount of information about its owner. And the FBI boasted the largest file of fingerprints on record anywhere. It was an agency to which Nick had been proud to belong. Leaving it had been a wrench, too. A woman with whom he'd been involved had been killed while he'd worked there. She, too, had been a special agent, infiltrating a counterfeiting ring. She'd been spotted and eliminated. That was how the supervisor had put it. Nick had been inconsolable and he'd quit the agency.

He wondered now if it hadn't been a case of simple loneliness and pity. The woman had needed someone at a time in Nick's life when he was feeling hopelessly alone. He'd almost turned to Tabby. But at that time, she'd been shy and introverted and he'd been sure that she would back away from any advance he made. She'd seemed to see him in only one light—that of a protective, affectionate older brother.

Obviously she hadn't seen him like that at the New Year's Eve party. His blood still ran hot at the memory of how eager she'd been for him. Now, having had time to adjust to seeing her in this unexpected way, he'd regretted pushing her away.

But years ago, he'd wanted Tabby. It had been because of that that he'd pursued the woman at work in the first place, out of a need to prove to himself that any woman would do. He didn't need a shy, nervous young woman who didn't even see him as a man.

Sometimes he thought Tabby was a bit afraid of him. The first move she'd ever made toward him had been at that party, when she'd had too much to drink. Apparently he was only palatable to her if she was too tipsy to think properly, and that was hardly flattering. If she'd ever wanted him in the old days, it had never shown. He was defensive toward her because it hurt his pride to think that he couldn't even attract a backward egghead like Tabby. Good God, she wasn't even pretty, and her figure left plenty to be desired. Why, then, he wondered angrily, did the memory of her body against his keep him awake at night? Why did her kisses haunt him?

Momentarily diverted when the elevator stopped, he strolled into one of the huge laboratories that peppered the building and grinned at the elderly form bent over a microscope. That familiar sight had greeted him every time he'd come here during his tenure as a special agent.

"Hello, Bartholomew," he greeted.

The old man looked up, and smiled with delight. "Nick! How nice to see you! Can you stay a while?"

"At least long enough to let you identify something for me," Nick teased. He shook hands with the amused laboratory chief. "How are you, Bart?"

"I've been better. When you get to my age, even arthritis is encouraging. It means you're still alive enough to feel pain!" He chuckled. "Why are you in town? Come home, are you? We could use a good special agent..."

"No. I'm on vacation. I'm working as a private detective these days. It's a little less fraught than working for the agency," he added with a chuckle.

"You look as if it agrees with you. What can I detect for you?"

"This." Nick pulled out the small plastic bag with the strand of hair. It looked odd now that he was out of the influence of Tabby and her snobbish boyfriend, and he scowled as he handed it over to Bart.

The older man lifted an eyebrow as he opened the bag and took out the sample. "Losing your touch, aren't you?"

Nick let out a sharp breath. "I must be. My God, that isn't human hair!"

"Bingo." Bart studied it and shrugged. "Animal fur. Someone has a dog, right?"

He wasn't sure if Tabby had one or not, but she'd mentioned going into the biology lab on the way over to the college. Probably she'd picked it up there, where they kept rats and mice and dogs and cats and such, and it had come off on her desk.

Nick took the sample back. "A dog or a rabbit or some such thing," he agreed. "Funny I didn't notice that it wasn't human."

"I can run it for you and tell you exactly what it is, if you like."

He shook his head. "No need. I'm getting careless, I guess," he said with a rueful smile.

"Something on your mind?"

"Yes. A lady," Nick replied. His broad shoulders rose and fell. "I'm sorry to have bothered you. There's been a theft. Nothing major, to my mind, but I'm trying to help a friend catch the culprit."

"If you come up with anything tangible, come back," Bart said with a twinkle in his eyes. "I don't get a lot of work these days. My eyes, you know. These younger boys and girls are taking over my old stomping ground." He stared at the test tubes and beakers and microscopes with a loving stare. "Don't get old, Nick."

"I'll do my best," he promised. He shook hands with the older man. "It was good to see you again," he said. "Sometimes I miss the old days."

"Don't we all. I didn't expect to hear from you again, after your own tragedy," he added sympathetically.

Nick nodded sadly. "It was a blow, losing her that way to a bullet. But I don't know that we'd ever have made a go of it. We were both career-minded, and she loved her work." He remembered the woman who'd filled the gaping hole Tabby had left in his life with fondness. He'd never loved Lucy, but he'd been fond of her. Her death had haunted him for years; now, he was finally able to face it.

The older man saw the bad memories in Nick's eyes and quickly changed the subject. "Say, remember that redhead who gave you fits when you first came here, the one who was transferred to Miami and we all got down on our knees and gave thanks?" he asked.

Nick chuckled. "Yes. What was her name... Cynthia something?"

"That's right. Well, she's chief agent in Miami these days," he told Nick. "Doing a helluva job, too. Married to one of her agents and has two kids."

"Imagine that," Nick said, shaking his head. "Funny, I never thought of her as a marrying woman."

"Neither did I. Sort of like you and me, Nick. I never found a woman I could live with. It doesn't look as if you ever did, either."

"I suppose some of us are born loners," Nick replied. Then he remembered Tabby's mention of Daniel as her fiancé and his eyes glittered with anger. He felt as if something was being taken from him. Ridiculous, of course. Tabby wasn't his.

The thing was, he couldn't get her out of his mind. All the way back to the college, he had her in his thoughts. It wouldn't do; it really wouldn't do.

Tabby wasn't in. He went by the admissions office and picked up a catalog. It gave some pretty detailed information about the faculty, and he could put that to good use. He strolled up to the floor where Tabby worked on the pretext of looking for her and got an earful from a janitor who was cleaning the hall. By the time he drove back to his parents' house, he had plenty of information to get him started on suspects.

He phoned the agency, and asked for his sister. She could get what he needed without involving any of the skip tracers. He didn't want everyone in the office knowing about his private life.

"What's up?" Helen asked.

"Tabby's career, if we don't find a thief," he said, and explained what he meant.

"But they wouldn't fire her, would they?" Helen asked worriedly. "I mean, she has tenure."

"That won't matter if that artifact doesn't turn up," he assured her. "I've got a list for you. Right at the top is her new 'fiancé.'"

"Daniel?" she asked pointedly, hiding a smile when Nick hesitated before confirming the guess.

"Do you know him?" he asked.

"Sure. He's my age, you know. He and Tabby and I were friends when we were all in college together. He's a bit of a stick in the mud, and I wouldn't call him exciting company. But he's nice, and settled. He'll take care of her."

"More than likely, she'll do the nurturing," he said shortly. "I don't like him. He's a prissy, self-centered snob."

"That, too," she agreed without heat. "It's Tabby's life, Nick. She's entitled to marry the man of her choice."

"Even if he's a rank idiot?" he asked coldly.

"Even then. Give me those names, will you, and I'll start checking. But you won't find anything shady in Daniel's past. He's much too straitlaced to have ever robbed a bank or anything."

"You never really know people until you dig deep," he assured her. "You know that. Got a pencil?"

"Yes. Go ahead."

He gave her the list of names and read her the appropriate information from the college catalog. "Get everything you can," he told her. "And phone me the minute you have anything concrete on any of these people."

"You can count on me, Bro," she agreed. "You might get some input from Tabby. Ask her if she suspects any of them," she said easily.

"That was my original idea," he said. "But I can't get her in the house. She's afraid her reputation will be ruined if people see her go into a house alone with me," he said irritably.

"She lives in an old-fashioned world," she told him. "She's not modern."

"I suppose not. It's so damned silly..."

"Humor her," Helen said. "Probably she's still raw about New Year's Eve. Tabby never drinks, and I really fouled things up for her by telling lies about your intentions," she added with quiet regret. "I was only trying to be a good scout, but I made her life miserable. She's probably embarrassed to be alone with you at all, in case you think she frequently gets drunk and throws herself at men."

"I know she isn't going to let history repeat itself, for heaven's sake," he said angrily. "She doesn't have to avoid me."

"Tell her."

He sighed roughly. "Maybe I should."

"Good man. Go to it. I'll get busy in the meantime. I'll give you a call when I find something. Bye."

She rang off and he put the receiver down. He wondered how long it would take Tabby to get home.

As it was, her car didn't pull into the driveway until dark. Nick watched her out the window, angry that she'd taken so long to come home, that she'd been out with her idiot fiancé. Tabby deserved better than that stuffed shirt. She was too good for him.

He went out and strolled over, just in time to open the door for her as she climbed out of her car with an armload of books.

"Oh. Thanks," she faltered. She hadn't expected to see him twice in the same day. Maybe he'd found out something. "Anything new?" she asked hopefully.

He shrugged. "Nothing yet. I'm working on it." He lifted the glass to his lips and caught her eyes on him. "It's whiskey and soda. Want some?"

She made a face. "I hate whiskey."

"You didn't mind it New Year's Eve. Did you?"

She flushed and turned toward her front door. "I have to get inside."

He caught her arm and held her back, so that her shoulder touched his broad chest in its thin shirt. She could feel the warmth, the maleness of him, and it made her ache.

"Don't, Nick," she pleaded gently.

"You did all the running that night," he accused at her ear. "Primped and swanned around me until all I saw was you. Then you plastered yourself against me in that black dress that fit you like a second skin and started kissing me." His body tautened with the memory. "I had to do something, quick, so I pushed you away and read you the riot act. But it was for your own good. You have to understand that it wasn't malicious on my part."

"I know that," she said, almost choking on wounded pride. "I'm engaged . . ."

"Oh, hell, he isn't an engagement, he's an ego trip. You only took up with him to prove to me that I was off the endangered list. Okay. I get the message. You don't have to shove it down my throat."

She turned, the heavy books clasped close to her breasts. "Nick, I'm not marrying Daniel to...to prove anything to you. I'm twenty-five. I want to settle down and have kids. Daniel is settled and he doesn't smoke or gamble or...drink," she added averting her eyes from his drink.

"I don't drink, either, as a rule," he said quietly, "and never to excess. I'm not driving, you notice," he added mockingly.

"Good thing," she murmured, grimacing at his breath. "You could probably fell an oak tree if you breathed on it. For heaven's sake, don't light a match."

"Funny girl," he said without humor. His eyes slid down to her vulnerable mouth and lingered there. "You still don't know how to kiss, do you?" he asked conversationally, ignoring her embarrassed start. "I should have taught you years ago, but you were afraid of me."

"I was not," she said defensively.

"You ran every time I came close," he challenged. "Once, I tried to ask you out. When you saw me coming, you left through the back door."

"I didn't know you wanted to take me anywhere," she said, avoiding his piercing stare. "You told Helen I was a pest and you wanted me out of your life. I got out."

He stood very still. "When was this?"

"That night you came over and asked to see me, when I was eighteen. I figured you planned to warn me off. I had a feeling that someone had told you how I, well, that I had a crush on you, and you were going to tell me it was no use. I didn't want to hear it, so I ran.''

He hadn't known about any crush. Helen hadn't told him anything. "Did Helen tell you that she'd said any such thing to me?'' he persisted.

"Oh, not Helen. She wouldn't have been so cruel. No. Mary Johnson told me. She said Helen had confided it to her. I was too embarrassed to say anything to either of you about it. I thought everything would be all right if I just kept out of your way. And it was.''

"I didn't tell anyone that you were a pest," he said through his teeth. "And I never knew about the crush. Maybe you don't know that Mary Johnson had an outsize yen for me and I had to slap her down, hard. She was one of your circle of friends, I recall.''

She stared down at her books. One of them had a creased cover. She traced it with her fingernail. "I thought she was my friend.''

"Apparently she was jealous of you.''

"Without cause.'' She sighed. "She said you hated the very sight of me, that I was too plain and dull to appeal to you.''

He didn't reply to that. He was trying to take it all in. So pretty little Mary had been the culprit who'd sent Tabby running from him all those years ago, passing lies to Tabby and keeping her at bay. What a travesty. Not that it would probably have mattered, because he wasn't any more ready for marriage then than he was now.

"For what it's worth, all these many years too late, I never thought of you as plain or dull. You had—still have—a keen, analytical mind and more than your fair share of intelligence.'' He smiled slowly. "You're not bad on the eyes, either. Not that you couldn't use a few more pounds."

"I don't eat much. I work hard."

"So do I." He drained his glass and stared at it. "Why Daniel?"

"Nobody else wanted me," she said involuntarily, and then felt stupid for having said such a thing. "I have to go in now, Nick," she added quickly. "I've got all this research to do for Daniel."

"Damn Daniel," he said carelessly. "Come home with me. I've got a new blues album we can dance to."

"You like blues?" she asked.

"Sure. Old-time blues, what they used to call torch songs."

"I like those, too."

"So Helen mentioned." He put his glass on top of her car and took the books from her grasp, despite her protests. He stuffed them back into the car, retrieved his glass, caught her by the hand and led her over to his house.

"It's dark. I can't," she began, pulling against his grasp.

He ignored her. A minute later, she was behind his closed door with him.

"I won't seduce you," he promised wickedly. "Not without fair warning. Come and have a drink with me while I put on the music."

"I don't drink and I'm not a good dancer..."

He ignored that, too. He put on the music, poured her a soda with a little whiskey in it and handed it to her. While she sipped it, he pulled her against his tall, fit body and began to move lazily to the rhythm while he drank from his own glass.

"You smell of gardenias," he said with lazy pleasure in the feel of her body against his. "I gave you a corsage of them once, remember?"

"When you took me to a class dance in college." She nodded. "I was the envy of every girl there, even though you only did it because Mary got Helen to ask you to."

He frowned. "She didn't."

"Mary said . . ." she protested.

He held her eyes. "Mary lied. Haven't you caught on yet? She wanted me. She was jealous of you."

"She was pretty."

"Plenty of women are. But I'm selective. Very, very selective. Right now," he murmured, bending close to her, "I have a raging hunger for tall brunettes with bow mouths."

She turned her face away and stiffened. "Don't tease me, Nick, please."

"You tasted of whiskey New Year's Eve night," he said huskily, his eyes still on her mouth. "You slid between my legs and moved on me as if you were born to be a siren, and I thought it was going to kill me to let you go. It damned near did. I wanted you."

"You didn't!" she protested, stopping to glare up at him. "You said horrible things to me!"

"It was that or take you to bed, and I wanted to," he said shortly. His eyes kindled. "You don't know how much I wanted to, Tabby. I could feel your body burning under those layers of cloth and I wanted to strip you down to your skin and make a banquet of you with my mouth."

She cleared her throat. "Shouldn't we sit down? It's rather warm in here."

"Isn't it, though." He moved her toward the mantel. Placing his glass on it, he took hers from her nerveless fingers and put it beside his. "Now," he said quietly.

He lifted her in his embrace as his mouth glided down to possess hers, its movements comforting, slow, encouraging a response that she'd rather have died than give him. But she couldn't resist. He tasted of whiskey and lime and his tongue was in her mouth, probing and teasing and withdrawing like a living thing. She moaned, trying to pull back while she still could.

"Don't fight it," he breathed. "Don't fight me. Open your mouth. Let me teach you how."

She tried to argue, but the motion of her lips only accommodated him more. She felt her body begin to sway toward him. He took instant advantage of that weakness, his hands pulling her hips gently into the thrust of his while he kissed her more and more deeply.

"Don't be afraid," he whispered as he bent and lifted her clear off the floor, his lips touching hers as he spoke. "I won't hurt you."

"Nick," she moaned weakly. But her hands were clinging, not fighting, and her body was on fire for him. It was the old need again, only this time he was giving her what only dreams had provided before. He was loving her, even if only physically.

"There's . . . Daniel," she tried to speak.

"Damn Daniel," he breathed roughly. "Make love to me."

She felt him place her on the long leather sofa. She felt his weight settling over her, pressing her down, consuming her. He was heavy and warm, and she loved the way he was kissing her, the way he was holding her. Daniel would never have presumed to touch her in such a way, to disregard the rules of conduct that she'd always expected.

Nick's hands accepted no restrictions. They smoothed over her taut breasts as if they had every right. They possessed her, made her ache with their expert caresses. His thumbs eased over the hard nipples and rubbed at them insistently, and he lifted his head to watch her reaction.

She gasped. He liked that, so he did it again. She trembled.

"Move up," he said quietly. When she did, he held her eyes while his knee insinuated itself between her thighs.

She stiffened, but he shook his head. "It's all right, Tabby," he said softly. "I'm only going to move a little closer. It isn't dangerous. I promise you, it isn't. Let me lie over you completely, little one. I can spare you most of my weight, like this..." He rested on his elbows as he eased down, and when she felt the intimacy of the movement, the arousal of his body, she cried out in mingled excitement and fear.

"This is overdue," he whispered unsteadily as his hips lowered. "Long, long overdue. Lie...still!"

Her last sane thought was that she was going to lose her chastity on a sofa. After that, nothing seemed to matter except pulling Nick as close as she could get him to the raging ache in her lower body. It gnawed so that it made her ache and cry out in her need. She'd never known sensations so urgent, so violent, that they pulsed through her like fire.

"Rock under me," he whispered quickly. "Yes. Yes! Lift up to me, Tabby...!"

She tried to, but her body was weak with need, with hunger. Her arms clung to him, gave in to him, while his mouth devoured hers with long, slow kisses that gave no relief at all.

His hand went under her, to force her hips up into the cradle of his. He moved rhythmically, feeling her body jerk as she accepted the intimacy, accepted the arousal of his body in an embrace he'd never meant to offer her.

"I want to have you," he said into her mouth, his body stiff and unsteady. "Are you protected? Is there a risk that I could make you pregnant?"

Risk. Pregnant. She opened her dazed eyes and looked at him. She was twenty-five and engaged to be married, and this man had already devastated her life once with his rejection. How had she managed to forget all that?

He moved involuntarily, and she remembered. Her face flamed as the intimacy they were sharing penetrated the delight he'd kindled in her.

"Nick?" she whispered unsteadily.

He lifted himself a little and looked down at her, at the position she was lying in beneath him. Her long legs were wrapped around his thighs and she was holding him low down on his back.

He smiled through his desire. "My, my," he said huskily. "I think you're getting the hang of this, Tabby."

She followed his gaze and abruptly moved her legs, pushing at him. "Let me go!"

"That isn't what you said five minutes ago," he replied lazily as he complied with her plea.

She tore out of his arms and got to her feet. Her legs would barely support her. Her hair was askew and hopelessly tangled. Her mouth was swollen. So were her breasts. He'd touched them through the fabric and they were tender. She felt . . . as she'd never felt in her life, and she didn't know how to handle it.

She stood over him, looking down at the length of his powerful, visibly aroused body and suddenly averted her gaze to his amused face.

"I'm not going to spare you by trying to hide it," he said. "I want you."

"I'm not . . . in the market for a love affair," she choked. "This isn't why I came home with you!"

"Isn't it?" he asked. He sat up lazily, his eyes acquisitive as they lingered on her soft body. "Are you going to try and pretend that you didn't feel anything?"

"I'm not that good an actress. I expect you could arouse a rock, with your experience," she said shortly. "But I'm not fair game. I'm engaged."

"Not for long," he said, "Not after I tell Daniel what we were doing on the sofa tonight."

"You wouldn't!" she exclaimed, horrified.

"I was having a good time until your conscience reared its ugly head," he said. "God knows why your body is living back in Victorian times when you have such a sensuous little mouth."

"Let's leave my sensuous mouth out of it," she said stiffly. "I have to go home. I've got work to do."

"You could come up to bed with me instead," he coaxed, his eyes soft and coaxing. "I could undress you and love you all night long. By morning, you couldn't remember Daniel's last name if your life depended on it."

"By morning, I'd be suicidal and you'd have a hangover and a guilty conscience that you led me on," she said coldly. "Just like New Year's Eve, when you accused me of everything from seduction to blackmail."

"You weren't ready for me then," he said quietly. "Now you are. That's the difference. I can give you something Daniel never will. I can satisfy you."

"I don't want you to satisfy me, thank you very much," she said stiffly. "I appreciate you helping me clear my name, but my body isn't going to be in lieu of salary. I hope that's understood."

"It is, but it's a hell of a shame," he sighed. "Money isn't half as sweet as you are when you let yourself go, Tabby."

"You were kidding, weren't you?" she asked at the door. "About telling Daniel, I mean."

He stared at her for a long moment. "Was I?" he asked softly.

She got out, quickly. He watched the closed door for one long moment before he poured himself another drink and went upstairs to take a long, very cold shower. Even so, it was hours before he finally slept. He hadn't realized just how potent Tabby would be. Now that he knew, he wondered if he was going to be able to forget.

He tossed and turned as the sensations he'd felt with Tabby racked his body. He slept nude, and the softness of the sheets was so much like the softness of her skin that he groaned out loud.

He got up finally and went to get himself a drink. It might not help, but it wouldn't hurt.

As he sipped it, he stood at his bedroom window and looked over at Tabby's house. He smiled slowly. Her bedroom light was on, too, so apparently she wasn't sleeping any better than he was.

She was such a contrast to Lucy. He could finally think about her without flinching. Lucy Waverly had been small and spicy and she'd liked to take risks. She liked long lovemaking sessions on the floor of his apartment, and she knew how to use her body as Tabby had never learned. Lucy had been exciting and a balm to his wounded masculinity after Tabby's rejection.

But love? No, he hadn't loved Lucy. He might have married her, just because of the excitement she gave him. But a bullet put paid to that proposition.

He'd gone to Lucy's funeral with dead eyes, and part of him had never been the same. He'd blamed himself for not marrying her and making her give up her job. Then, after a year, he got realistic and came to the conclusion that he could no more have deprived her of the job she loved than she could have deprived him of it.

Lucy was gone and he had to face the world without her. But he thought about the way she'd died, and the risks of his own job. That had kept his later liaisons brief and unemotional.

Tabby was changing all that. She was winding herself around him with her eccentric little ways and her soft, sweet mouth. She was killing him with remembered pleasure.

He wasn't sure what was going to happen, and he didn't want any commitment. But he did want Tabby. If he could induct her into the modern world, and get her out of her Victorian attitudes, what an affair they could have! He had erotic visions of Tabby's eager body in bed with him while he took her from frightened virgin to sated woman.

The prospect was so delicious that he barely slept the rest of the night for dreaming about it.

Four

Nick was drowsy and out of sorts when he dragged himself from the bed. He felt hung over from frustration as well as alcohol. He, who seldom drank, had certainly made some inroads into the meager supply of scotch whisky he kept at the house.

It was Sunday. He hadn't been to church in some years. Now he felt the need to go again, to be with Tabby. That need sent him right back to bed, and he slept without interruption until midafternoon.

Eventually he drank enough black coffee and took enough aspirins to get his mind back together. He phoned Helen to see if she'd had time to find out any morsel of information. He half hoped she hadn't. He didn't relish the thought of seeing Tabby after the fool he'd made of himself the night before. He seemed to have this crazy compulsion to lead her on, when he had nothing, not a damned thing, to offer her. He didn't want her permanently. Why couldn't he manage to leave her alone? It would be in her best interests, and certainly in his. But every time he thought of her, his toes curled.

He really wouldn't tell precious Daniel what they'd done together the night before, but it did serve to keep Tabby guessing when he threatened it.

She'd been so sweet wrapped around him like that. He remembered her long, silky legs sliding against his and his body violently protested the memory.

He got up and paced the floor, trying to calm the heat in his loins. Nothing seemed to work. Bedtime finally came. He'd wasted a whole day being miserable. He wondered if Tabby had, too, or if she'd had other things on her mind. He noticed a strange white car in her driveway for most of the afternoon and knew without being told that it had to be Daniel. Damn Daniel, he thought as he went up to bed. The man was driving him crazy.

So was Tabby.

He got up early the next day and went over to Tabby's kitchen, knocking on the door as soon as he saw the lights go on.

Tabby opened the kitchen door sleepily. She was so sleepy, in fact, that she didn't seem to realize she was standing there in a thigh-length soft cotton nightshirt that revealed every line and curve of her body. With her hair long around her shoulders and her face flushed from sleep, she was enough to arouse a statue—which Nick wasn't.

She realized suddenly what she'd done, but it was too late. Nick moved toward her with intent.

Quickly she got a kitchen chair between them and held it there, blocking him.

"Now, Nick," she said, laughing nervously. "You just remember that you're a confirmed bachelor. Repeat it several times."

"I have. It doesn't help. Move the chair, Tabby," he said huskily.

He did look sexy with his shirt half unbuttoned, his sleeves rolled up. His hair was just disheveled enough to give him a rogueish look. His dark eyes twinkled with amusement and frank desire as he tried to go around the chair.

She blocked him again. "No good, Nick," she commented. "I'm a dried-up spinster living in the cobwebs. Isn't that what you told Helen after you left here at New Year's?"

He stopped dead. "She wouldn't have said that to you," he began.

"She thought she was doing me a favor, actually," Tabby replied, and she looked faintly wounded. "I'd cried all night long and she thought I was going to die eating my heart out for you, if she didn't tell me the truth. In the long run, it was best, Nick."

"I never knew how you felt about me when you were in school," he said, his voice deep and quiet in the kitchen. The only other noise was the faint whirr of the washing machine on the utility porch. "You ran the other way so much that you bruised my ego."

"I'm sorry. I was shy of you," she said. "Much too shy to do anything or say anything blatant." Her face lifted proudly. "But that's all in the past, Nick. I'm engaged to Daniel. I'm going to be married."

His dark eyes narrowed. "You don't love Daniel."

"I respect and like him," she said. "At my age, that's no bad thing. I can live without passion. It's like flashfire—easily kindled and just as easily put out."

He got the message at once. "And what you felt with me on my sofa last night was just flashfire?"

She nodded, schooling her face not to give her away. "Just that. Overdue passion, a residue from my hero-worshiping days. I wanted to know how it would feel if you made love to me. Now my curiosity is satisfied."

"Not completely," he said, his face arrogant and hard. "Why don't you go to bed with me and get a complete picture?"

Her face flooded with heat, but she shook her head. "Too drastic. A taste was enough."

"That was more than a taste."

She cleared her throat. "Nick, I have to get dressed and get to work."

Work. He remembered that he was supposed to be working, too, and on her case. He'd allowed himself to get sidetracked the night before because of his hunger for her. He couldn't afford the luxury today.

"Yes. So do I." His eyes ran down over her body. He wondered what her breasts looked like under that cotton. They seemed to rise without support, and he remembered how warm and firm they'd felt in his hands the night before. "Take it off and let me look at you," he said huskily, catching her gaze. "I want to see you without your clothes, Tabby."

His voice was as seductive as his eyes, but Tabby had enough will to save herself from that final humiliation. Nick wanted her. Men could be devious when their needs were involved. But once he'd actually possessed her, it would be the end because he couldn't make a commitment. She'd be agreeing to nothing more than a delicious but quickly forgotten one-night stand on his part. The thought made her sad.

"I'm sure you've said the same thing to half a dozen other women over the years, Nick," she replied. "Sorry. I don't do striptease work. Just anthropology."

"Ancient work does rather go with ancient attitudes, doesn't it?" he asked sharply.

She shrugged. "I wasn't raised to be licentious. You weren't either, but I guess your early education didn't take, did it?"

He glared at her. "I'm not locked up in outdated myths and morals."

"To each his own," she said without heat. "Go home, Nick. I'm busy."

"You still look a little hung over this morning," he told her dryly. "Wouldn't Daniel have a screaming fit if he knew why?"

"Daniel wouldn't have a screaming fit if I had sex with a martian on my front lawn," she replied imperturbably. "He's an intelligent man. He'd understand."

"Think so? We could find out."

"Why bother?" she asked with a faint frown. "Nick, you don't want me, really. You've discovered years too late that I had a crush on you, and maybe you were as curious as I was. But that's all it is. You don't have the slightest temptation to settle down and have children."

He stuck his hands deep in his pockets and his eyes grew thoughtful as he stared at her. "No," he said honestly. "I don't. But if I ever did want a family, I think I'd want it with you."

She smiled. "I'm very flattered."

He shrugged. "I'm footloose. I don't suppose I'll ever be able to stay in one place very long. I like de-

tective work, police work. I like the challenge and the
danger. That doesn't really mix with a settled life-style.
And I can't imagine watching you go out of your mind
wondering when I might end up in a hospital somewhere because I poked my nose into the wrong pot."

"If you loved me, I might risk it," she said. "But
love isn't a word you know."

"It never will be," he said. "Dodging bullets is one
thing. Being at the mercy of a woman is another."

She knew what he was telling her. He never in-
tended letting a woman close enough to hurt him.
She'd heard rumors about his lady love at the FBI
getting killed, and that he'd never gotten over it. Hel-
en, and Mary, had told her. He probably never would
get over it. She couldn't go on tormenting herself with
hope that he'd care about her one day. Helen was right
on that score. It was better to go ahead and marry
someone and settle down.

"You're independent," she said. "I know how that
feels. But I'm tired of living alone and depending on
myself. Daniel and I get along very well. We'll have a
good life together."

"Sure," he said easily. "As long as you don't have
to suffer him too often in bed."

She colored. "I beg your pardon!"

"Don't sound so starchy. If Daniel could satisfy
you, I wouldn't have had such an easy time of it last
night. You were ready for me the second I touched
you. You don't want him at all, physically, do you?"

"Sex isn't everything!"

"Marriages stand and fall on it, or so I'm told," he
countered. "If you don't want him, Tabby, your life
is going to be hell. He'll know it, and hate you for it."

She couldn't admit that Daniel already found her stiffness unappealing. Her lack of response to his infrequent kisses irritated him.

"I'll get used to that part of it."

"Get used to it! My God!"

"I'd rather have a man I can talk to... Nick!"

He'd torn the chair out of her hands while she was still speaking. Seconds later he had her back down on the kitchen table, and his mouth was on hers.

She couldn't struggle. The slick Formica top made her position precarious, so that if she moved she was in danger of sliding off. Nick held her down with one big, lean hand while his mouth ravaged hers. She gave in helplessly, almost hating him for the ease of his conquest.

His hand slid down over her breast to her stomach and then to the top of her thigh. He eased the hem of her nightie up, very slowly, making her all too aware that there was nothing under it.

All the while, she looked up at him with wide, shocked eyes that couldn't see beyond the intense pleasure his mouth had given her, the feel of his warm, deft hand on her body.

His fingers trailed up her silky thigh. She caught her breath and shivered. She should catch his hand and stop it. She should protest. But all she did was lie there, at his mercy, waiting.

His dark eyes slid down to the hem of the nightshirt. Under it, his hand had found the soft apex of her hip and her thigh and was resting there.

She felt the caress in every pore of her body. Her legs felt boneless, her heart throbbed. Her lips parted as the lingering touch made her ache and swell.

"You aren't wearing briefs," he whispered. "Do you always sleep like this?"

"Yes," she whispered huskily.

"And always alone?"

"Always."

His hand flattened on her body, teasing, tormenting. If he moved it a few inches, it would promote an intimacy she'd never experienced. Part of her wanted that, wanted to know passion. Another part was afraid, shy, inhibited.

"You're tense," he said softly. "So tense. It isn't necessary. I wouldn't hurt you for anything in the world. Don't you know that?"

"Yes."

His hand moved slowly up her body until it found the taut, high swell of her breast. He touched her there, feeling her stiffen and catch her breath. His thumb and forefinger drew circles around the taut nipple, making her squirm.

"I've already seen you in my dreams," he whispered. Both hands went to the bottom of the nightshirt. "Now, I'm going to make them come true for both of us."

He eased the fabric up her body until it came to rest, finally, bunched up under her chin. He looked at her and caught his breath, while she lay there, flushed and hungry under his eyes.

"My God," he said through his teeth. "Tabby, you're exquisite!"

His eyes told her that she was desirable, even before his head bent and his mouth worshiped her breasts. She arched upward, welcoming his warm lips, his tongue, his teeth as he made a meal of her. His mouth was pressing down hard on her belly when the telephone rang and kept ringing.

He lifted his mouth from her body and stared at her, not quite rationally.

"It's the telephone," he said huskily.

"It isn't stopping," she murmured dazedly.

He gave her one long, last look. His lean hands smoothed over her body with possession, leaving a trail of pleasure where they touched. "I thought you were thin," he whispered ruefully. His mouth teased around her breasts and kissed the hard tips with a warm, torturous suction that made her pulse with new hunger. "I want to make love to you," he breathed. "I want you to lie under me and let me take you."

"Nick!" she wailed.

He stood erect all at once, his eyes dark and possessive for several seconds before he pulled her off the table and jerked her nightshirt down to cover the body his mouth had explored so tenderly.

"You'd better answer it," he said curtly.

She picked it up with trembling hands. "Hello?"

"Tabby, it's nine o'clock," Daniel said impatiently. "Your class is waiting for you."

She gasped. "Daniel, I'm sorry! I...overslept," she said with a flushed glance at Nick. "I'll be right there. Can you sub for me for a few minutes? I'm going over physical anthropology and its technical terms—you know those as well as I do."

"All right," he said. "You're lucky my next class isn't until ten."

"Thank you! You're a lifesaver!"

She hung up and pushed back her disheveled hair.

"Forget the class and come to bed," Nick said, his body still throbbing with hunger.

"I can't," she whispered. "Even if I didn't have a class. Nick, you have to stop doing this to me! I can't handle it!"

He smiled slowly. "You want me."

"Of course I want you! But there's no future in it!"

His broad shoulders shifted as he leaned against the table. "We could still enjoy each other, while it lasted," he said seriously. "I wouldn't hurt you."

"I'm engaged," she repeated.

"To a fool," he scoffed. "He's only using you."

"What are you trying to do?" she exclaimed.

He didn't like the way that sounded. "If you want to put it like that, we'd be using each other. I need a woman. You need a man. We've got a long past behind us, and we like each other."

"You're describing what I have with Daniel as well," she said stiffly. "I'd like you to leave, Nick."

"No, you wouldn't," he replied, his eyes going like homing pigeons to her sharp-tipped breasts. "You're still as hungry as I am."

"But I'm back in my right mind now," she said. "I won't be unfaithful to Daniel."

"That comes after marriage, not before."

"Not in my world," she replied. "I haven't become cynical, Nick. I still have my golden ideals. I believe in happy marriages and long relationships."

"Relationships don't last. You're as big a fool as your Daniel if you don't know that by now."

"All I know is that I've got a better chance for happiness with Daniel than I have with you," she said, exasperated. "Please go."

"If you insist." He pushed away from the table and opened the back door. "I've got Helen doing some checking for me. The offices were closed yesterday.

She'll have something for me later this morning, I hope." He stared at her. "I'll need access to your office today. I have a couple of people I want to interview."

"You won't start any trouble?" she asked nervously.

"I'm a trained private investigator," he said angrily. "I have a degree in law."

"Sorry."

"I know you're nervous about being accused of something you didn't do, but if it takes stepping on a few toes to clear you, I don't mind doing it."

"I just don't want to make any more enemies than I have to," she said.

"I'm aware of that."

"Nick, how do you know I'm innocent of the charges?" she asked seriously.

"Because I know you," he said, surprised by the question. "I'll see you at the college, Tabby."

Later, he wondered himself why he'd never doubted her innocence. Perhaps it was a form of telepathy, but he was certain that he'd know if she lied to him. Certainly she was lying about her feelings for Daniel. Seeing her with the man had convinced Nick that she couldn't be in love with him. There was no spark between them, no hint of romantic interest, no physical attraction.

Between himself and Tabby, it was a totally different story. He wanted her desperately. After this morning, it was going to be hell trying to keep away from her at all.

She had the most beautiful, desirable body he'd ever seen. He wanted all of it, all of her. But her price was just too high for him to pay.

* * *

Nick went to Thorn College and set up his interrogations in Tabby's office while she was teaching her classes. Dr. Flannery, the assistant biology professor, was high on his list of suspects. One of the few things he'd learned about the man was that he needed money, and that he'd been accused of theft while still in his teens. Tabby's fiancé, meanwhile, had been arrested for taking part in an antiwar demonstration back in the sixties and had spent some time in jail. He'd deliberately falsified information on his record to that effect.

The computer in Tabby's office gave out a wealth of information on the faculty. Helen, one of the finer hackers in the Western Hemisphere, had supplied Nick with the password that got him into the college's personnel files. He was having a field day going through them. There was only one other suspicious person on the staff, and that was Dr. Day. Day was over the art department, and something of a professional layabout before, during and after college. He seemed to always have money, but the things he owned didn't jibe with the salary he was paid to teach. The Lamborghini, for instance, was a bit above the average college professor's salary.

Nick narrowed his investigation down to those three men, and proceeded to carefully and warily dig out any information he could about them. He discovered, not to his amazement, that Daniel was the only one of the three whom most everyone on campus disliked. Daniel soon became his number one suspect, but Nick had to keep his suspicions to himself for the time being. Tabby might not even believe his accusations, or she'd attribute them to jealousy,

He couldn't blame her. His behavior had been erratic and unbelievable, even to himself. He'd sworn to keep away from her, but more and more he was getting in over his head with her physically. One dark night, he thought irritably, he was going to steal into her bedroom and seduce her. That would certainly complicate an already impossible situation. She was bent on avoiding him after their interlude at her home. He sighed as he worked. Back to square one. It was no less than he'd expected.

Meanwhile, Tabby was trying to come to grips with her behavior of the morning. Allowing herself to be bent back over a kitchen table and fondled like some harem girl didn't sit well on her conscience. Ever since he'd come back, Nick had gone out of his way to make her aware of him. He'd been almost jealous of her relationship with Daniel, and frankly protective.

That was flattering, but it wasn't love. It wasn't even something permanent. Nick was on a case and she was handy. Perhaps he hadn't had a woman in a long time. She wished she knew more about his late woman friend.

During a slack period during the morning, she called Helen just to talk, because she wanted to do a little prying of her own.

"How's Nick doing?" Helen asked.

"All right, I suppose, he's very close-lipped about what he's finding out. Helen," she added slowly. "Tell me about Lucy."

"Ah. I was wondering if you'd ever ask," the other woman said gently. "Nick started going with her just after you turned down that skiing trip with us."

Tabby's heart skipped. "You asked me . . ."

"On his behalf. I even told you he'd wanted you along, but I guess he'd rejected you so much by then that you didn't believe anything he said. I'm sorry."

Tabby tangled the telephone cord around her finger and watched it curl. "So am I. Nick said that Mary had told me a lot of lies."

"Mary!" Helen ground out. "Yes, she did, and I knew nothing about it until you'd gone off to college and she laughed about breaking up your crush on Nick. She wanted him herself, but he didn't want her. It was pure malice. I wish I'd known."

"She didn't get him," Tabby said with quiet satisfaction.

"No, she didn't," Helen said curtly. "She wound up with a bald banker twenty years her senior and the last time I saw her she looked older than he did. She hasn't had a good life."

"Poor Mary," Tabby said.

"Poor you," came the reply. "If it hadn't been for Mary, you might be married to Nick by now."

"Not likely. He isn't the marrying kind, is he?"

"I don't know. I think he was, before Lucy got killed, but her death frightened him. He learned that it hurt to lose people you cared about, even if they weren't people you loved. He's afraid to risk his heart. Especially," she added thoughtfully, "on someone he could love obsessively. He's growled about you ever since we were here the first of the year. But he hasn't been the same, either."

"I . . . noticed that he's less brittle."

"Our Nick?" Helen chuckled. "Pat yourself on the back. He's been breakable out here."

"It's the case. I don't flatter myself that it's me. He enjoys a good mystery."

"Is that all he's enjoying?" came the bland reply.

Tabby remembered his eyes on her nudity that morning and blushed to the roots of her hair. "What was Lucy like?" she asked, putting the knife into her own heart with the question.

"Dainty and beautiful and devil-may-care. She burned like a candle flame, and went out just as easily. She was reckless and liked taking risks, just like Nick." Helen paused, because she was thinking, as Tabby was, how he liked risk and how easily he put his life on the line. He could wind up just like Lucy with no trouble at all. It was a frightening thought.

"Did he love her?" Tabby asked.

"He was fond of her. I think he found her exciting and sensual, and I'm pretty sure they were having a hot affair. He mentioned marriage, but without any real enthusiasm. I've never said this to him, but I always had the feeling that he would have broken it off in the end. He wasn't committed to her, even if he did find her vividly desirable."

"I suppose...women like that appeal to sophisticated men like Nick," Tabby said dully.

"In bed, sure." Helen laughed. "But not as prospective wives. Nick was raised to believe in all the virtues, even if he doesn't practice them. He'll settle one day, but it won't be with some vivid butterfly who likes the social life. He'll want a pipe and an easy chair and his children on his lap at bedtime to read stories to. You mark my words, he's got all the makings of a family man. He just doesn't know it yet."

"I wish..." Tabby began fervently.

"Don't give up on him," Helen said gently. "I know I tried to put you off him for your own good, but he's changed since January. He really has. Give it a chance."

"He wants me," she blurted out.

"Good. That's a step in the right direction. Just don't give in to him. That's the best way I know to classify yourself with his other women and turn him away."

"I know that. But it's hard," she confessed. "I do love him so, Helen."

"So do I," his sister admitted. "I think he's pretty special. But, then, so are you, my friend. Keep in touch. And don't brood, about Nick or the spot you're in. It will all work out. Really, this time next year, you'll hardly remember it."

"I hope you're right," Tabby said. But long after she put the receiver down, she remained unconvinced.

Five

There was a crowd in the halls when Nick came out of Tabby's office after having used the computer at Thorn College.

Shrieks were coming from the biology lab, and the outer door was open. With assumed casualness, he walked in.

Dr. Flannery was trying to calm a violently upset Pal. The man was holding something in his hands that the primate was obviously bent on possessing.

"You can't have these!" he was telling the monkey. "Where did you get them, anyway?"

"What does he have?" Nick asked with amused interested.

Dr. Flannery looked over his shoulder and his pink complexion went even pinker. "Dr. Day's keys," he replied. "God knows where he found them. Dr. Day must have been in here earlier."

"Are you teaching him to steal now, Flannery?" Daniel asked from the door with that maddeningly superior tone that put everyone's back up.

"I am not!" Flannery choked, and went even redder. "Would you give these to Dr. Day at lunch, please?" he asked Daniel, handing him the keys. "I have a meeting."

"Glad to," Daniel replied. "That animal's a born thief. I'd watch him if I were you."

"That's what I'm trying to do."

"This primate project is a waste of time," Daniel muttered. "The only thing you're going to learn about that creature is that he's adept at sleight of hand."

"I believe your field is history?" Dr. Flannery asked pointedly.

Daniel shrugged. "It doesn't take a biologist to recognize an animal with a bad attitude." He glanced with irritation at Nick, who'd been leaning against the door facing, taking in the conversation. "Did you need something, Mr. Reed?"

"Only Tabby," Nick replied with a sensuality in his tone that penetrated even Daniel's thick skull.

Daniel seemed to grow an inch. "My fiancée," he stressed the word, "is teaching her class."

"I know." Nick shouldered away from the wall. "Nice of you to take her class until she got here."

"How did you know that?" the older man demanded.

Nick smiled slowly. "Why don't you ask Tabby?" He turned and walked along the hall, intent for the moment on finding Dr. Day.

The art department was in a separate building, and it took some searching before he found Dr. Day's class. The interested looks he was getting from some of the women students amused him. But lately, the only face he saw was Tabby's. Who'd have believed that she had a body like that, he wondered as he walked along. Her clothes made her look thin and lackluster. But under them . . . He groaned silently at the memory of how it had been to look at her, to touch and taste her. He wanted her more and more every day, and that wouldn't do.

He found Dr. Day in a corner classroom, just gathering his things together into an attaché case. He was a tall, thin man with thick dark hair, and he looked faintly nervous.

"Dr. Day?" Nick introduced himself and shook hands with the other man. "I hope you don't mind. I'm trying to find out as much as I can about a recent theft."

"You think I'm involved?" he asked, immediately defensive.

"Good heavens, no," Nick drawled. "I wanted to know if you had any idea why someone might stoop to the theft of an ancient relic in the anthropology department, that's all."

Day relaxed, but only a little. He kept shoveling papers into that attaché case, but now his long fingers were trembling. "Why does anyone steal?" he asked. "For monetary gain."

"There are other motives."

He glanced at Nick. "Professional jealousy, I suppose?" He nodded. "Well, just between us, Dr. Daniel Myers has more than his share of that. He and Dr. Harvey were once what you might call serious rivals even though they work in different departments. They're engaged now, though, so I assume that they've settled their differences."

"Dr. Myers has your car keys, by the way." Nick told him after they'd talked for a few minutes. "He'll give them to you at lunch."

"What is Dr. Myers doing with my car keys?" he asked irritably.

"Dr. Flannery's primate research project took them, I understand."

"That blasted monkey! I wish someone would cook and eat him. He's a positive menace!"

"Most of the faculty on his floor would tend to agree with you." Nick frowned. "How did your keys get into the biology lab, if you don't mind my asking?"

"I haven't been in the biology lab in two days," Dr. Day replied seriously. "The last time I remember having my keys was in the audiovisual room. That's in the library, next door to the main building where the biology lab is temporarily located."

"Surely the monkey can't leave the building when he wants to?"

"He can pick locks, didn't you know?" Day scoffed. "The damned thing's almost human. That's what scares me. One morning they'll find him in the dean's office smoking cigars and drinking brandy. Then where will Flannery's precious research funds go?"

He seemed to find that thought amusing. Nick thanked him and made a few more stops on his way around the campus. Then he went back to find Tabby, because it was now nearing the lunch hour.

She and Daniel were in her office, in the middle of a heated discussion.

"It wasn't like that at all," she was saying. "Daniel, you can't believe . . . !"

"What else can I believe? And isn't his arrival right now a little convenient?" he added narrowly. "My God, you almost drool when he walks into a room! I've had no input from you in days about our book. I can't even get you on the telephone in the evenings. And this morning you're late and he knows that you asked me to take your class. How?"

"Go ahead, honey. Tell him," Nick dared her, pausing in the doorway.

Tabby flushed. "Don't make it sound like that!"

"Why not?" he returned. "It *was* like that." His eyes went to her blouse and lingered until she flushed. "I'm the reason she was late," he told Daniel, and he smiled.

Daniel went scarlet with rage. He glared at Tabby. "So that's what's going on. And you said it was just an old crush. But that's not true. You're lovers, aren't you?"

"No!" Tabby gasped.

"Conspirators, too, probably," Daniel continued angrily. "I don't doubt that you're guilty of that theft after all, Tabitha, and that you did it to discredit me! You know that when Brown retires, I'm in line for a promotion to head of the history department. You can't stand it that I might achieve a higher position than you have in the sociology department, isn't that it?"

"Daniel, you aren't even making sense!" she exclaimed. "Stealing an important find would only discredit me!"

"I'm engaged to you, so it would discredit me as well!" he shot back. "I must have been out of my mind to propose to you!"

He walked out, still fuming. Nick's dark eyes never left Tabby's white face. "I don't think you did it," he reminded her.

She looked limp. "Thanks, Nick. For that," she added, glaring at him wearily, "*not* for making Daniel think we're lovers."

"We'd be lovers if you were a little less rigid," he said easily. "Come on. I'll buy you lunch."

She was too tired to argue. Besides, there was little danger of any more romantic interludes in a public place.

Or so she thought. But Nick had other ideas in mind. He bought a picnic lunch from a fried chicken franchise and herded her into the nearby park, to a secluded area under a sprawling oak tree.

"Isn't this nice?" he asked while they ate warm chicken.

"Peaceful, at least," she agreed. If it hadn't been quite so isolated, she'd have minded less. A stream flowed through and the gurgling of the water sounded quite close, mingled with the singing of birds in the trees around them.

"You could use a little peace after your morning."

"Why did you have to let Daniel know you were with me when he called?" she asked miserably.

"Why try to hide it?" he countered. "He doesn't own you. My God, you don't even want him. He's only using you to further his own career. A blind woman could see that, but apparently you can't."

"Why he wants me didn't matter at the time," she confessed. "I only wanted..."

"To spite me," he said for her, his dark eyes narrowing as he finished a third piece of chicken. He wiped his hands and mouth on a napkin before he took a sip of coffee from a paper cup. "Maybe to show me that you could get married if you wanted to. I slapped you down hard on New Year's Eve. I don't blame you for doing something outlandish."

"I was drunk!"

He looked at her solemnly. "No. You wanted me. And I didn't want you."

"I know that, you don't have to rub it in," she said in a ghostly tone, averting her eyes to her own cup of coffee.

He studied her, approving the way she looked in the prim green-and-white pattern shirtwaist dress she was wearing. Her hair was bundled up on top of her head with a green scarf. She looked younger than usual, and very flustered.

He smiled, lounging back against the tree. He'd removed the sports coat that went with his dark brown slacks, and his tie with it. His white shirtsleeves were rolled up, the throat of his shirt unbuttoned. His hair was windblown and he looked reckless and elegant, lying there.

"I didn't realize how potent you'd be if we ever started kissing, until that night," he continued. "I was curious about you years ago, but every time I made a move, you backed away."

"You never made any moves," she countered.

"But I did. I can remember one particular instance, when I invited you to come up to law school for the weekend and go to a party with me."

Her dark eyes met his. "You were teasing. You laughed even when you said it."

"And you blushed and mumbled something and rushed off," he agreed. "I was serious. I meant it."

"I'm sure you didn't have any shortage of partners," she said stiffly.

"No. But it was you I wanted. You made me ache when you were eighteen, Tabby," he said softly. "I noticed you without any effort at all. But you were painfully shy of me. When I went to work for the FBI, I tried again, but that was a disaster. I ran to Lucy in self-defense, to prove to myself that I was still a man."

Her breasts rose and fell heavily with a long sigh. "They said you never got over her death."

"It was unexpected," he said. "And I was fond of her. We got along well enough. I might have married her eventually." He searched Tabby's sad face. "But she was the consolation prize, nothing more. A substitute for what I really wanted and couldn't have." He sat up suddenly, holding her eyes. "Haven't you worked it out? I've spent years telling myself that you found me too frightening to touch. Then New Year's Eve, you launched yourself on me and started kissing me, and I couldn't get away from you fast enough. I couldn't believe that you really wanted me. I thought it was a drunken aberration."

"It was!"

He shook his head. "No." He lay back again and opened his arms. "Come here."

She froze, her lips trembling as she fought the temptation.

"Come on," he coaxed, smiling.

Her eyes widened. "I won't," she choked.

"Not enough temptation for you?" He paused to unbutton his shirt, watching her eyes go homing to the thick pelt of hair on his strongly muscled chest as he tore the shirt away from it and let her look. "Now, come here," he challenged softly, and held out his arms again.

She went to him against her better judgment. He pulled her down on him and found her mouth with slow passion, opening it to the soft probe of his tongue.

She caught her breath and he felt it, and smiled. He eased her over, onto her back and while he kissed her, his hand gently took the soft weight of her breast and caressed her as if she belonged to him.

"Touch me," he whispered roughly.

Her hands slid up and down over the thick hair, the warm muscle of him. She loved the way he felt, the faint throb of his heartbeat gaining strength under her fingertips. The breeze blew gently and bird songs filled the air while she heard her own quick breathing, and Nick's, magnified in the stillness.

She was dazed with pleasure when she felt his hand guiding hers away from his chest, down over the firm muscles of his stomach, until she touched him where his passion for her was most visible.

Her hand jerked away, but he pressed it there, and his mouth became hot and insistent on her parted lips. For one long, exquisite moment, she gave in to her need and his, and let him teach her.

The intimate feel of his body had an unexpected effect on her. She burned with the need to satisfy his hunger, to give him peace. She wanted him to touch her as she was touching him, she wanted him to pull her dress away and kiss her bare body. She wanted to be under him, over him, wanted to absorb him as earth absorbs water...

She didn't realize that she was whispering it to him, telling him all her secrets, her voice breaking as her hand pressed harder against him, learning him.

He groaned and moved suddenly, his weight between her lax thighs, the press of his aroused flesh suddenly intimately demanding. She cried out at the sensations it gave her when she felt him as she'd never experienced a man in her life.

"Nick...we...can't!" she gasped.

But he didn't hear her. The area was completely isolated, deserted. His hands were under her skirt, touching her, paving the way. She heard a faint rasp and then felt him without any hint of fabric in the way.

"Nick!" she cried out.

"It's all right," he choked at her ear. His hands gentled her, trembling, as he eased closer, probing. He caught his breath and groaned helplessly. "Oh, God, Tabby, let me! Baby, let me, let...me!"

His mouth covered hers with aching tenderness while he pushed down in a feverish, mindless agony of need. She cried out, because it was difficult. But seconds later, she felt him completely possess her, and she gasped at the incredible sensations she felt when he began to move with a slow, deliberate rhythm.

He kissed her while he loved her, his tongue imitating what his body was doing. He rocked over her, his body slow and unsteady, but very expert as he drew pleasure from her. He whispered to her, his voice unsteady, broken with pleasure, coaxing her to move, to lift, to absorb him.

The rhythm was unbelievably arousing. She jerked as the sensations shot through her like swelling fire, made her body wanton, made her brain shut down completely. There was only Nick, and the heat of his possession, the sharp urgency of his movements, the pleasure he was building and building until she tensed with an anguish bordering on madness.

She heard him repeating her name as his movements suddenly became violent. The world exploded around her, inside her. She cried out and began to convulse helplessly in hot contractions that were as frightening as they were ecstatic.

He shuddered and cried out in hoarse ecstasy, his body arching over her, his face clenched with the unbearable sweetness that racked his powerful body. Eons later, he slowly collapsed on her and lay still and spent, shivering with exhaustion even as she reached the most incredible peak of sensation. She couldn't breathe, couldn't bear it! She whispered it brokenly, her nails digging into his hips, pleading with him.

He gathered her closer and put his mouth over hers, rocking on her body until she convulsed again, and again. She cried out and her eyes opened, looking straight into his and his face blurred into red waves of delight.

She came back to awareness a little later, and her body felt cold and sick. They weren't even undressed. He'd only moved the most necessary things out of the way. He'd made love to her, taken her completely, in a public park under a tree where anyone could have seen them. The fact that the park was completely deserted made no difference. It was shameful and disgusting.

She began to cry. Vaguely she heard Nick's apology, felt him rearranging her disheveled clothing, righting his own. He pulled her up and into his arms, and held her cradled against him, his face a study in remorseful anguish.

"I lost it," he said, as if he still couldn't quite believe what he'd done. "My God, Tabby, I lost it! I'm sorry. Baby, I'm so sorry!"

She cried even harder. It wasn't just the loss of her chastity, it was the knowledge that to him it was just another casual interlude. It was also the shame of where it had happened. She was just like those women who walked the streets and sold their bodies, she thought hysterically. She had no morals!

He dried her eyes, but she wouldn't meet his concerned gaze. She drew away from him and got to her feet, surprised at how shaky she felt.

"Do you want me to take you home?" he asked slowly.

"I want to go back to work," she said shakily. "I'll... I'll..."

He caught her shoulders and turned her to face him. "I hurt you."

She tore away from him, horribly embarrassed, and began to run. He caught up with her easily, but she wouldn't look at him. Tears filled her eyes, her world.

"I'll drive you home," he said shortly. "You need a shower at least. Maybe a doctor..."

"I don't need a doctor!"

"All right," he said quietly. "Come on."

They drove to her house in silence. She phoned the college and told them she'd been delayed and would be right back. It didn't matter what they thought. Daniel had as much as said he didn't want to marry her anymore. That was just as well, because she was a loose woman. Nick's woman. Nick's... lover. There was no question of her ever being anything else, because he wanted no part of marriage.

She went quickly to her bedroom and laid out clean clothes, then into the shower. She felt only marginally better when she was wearing slacks and a gray silk top, with fresh makeup. But finding Nick pacing the living room didn't help her morale, or her feelings.

"Ready to go?" he asked stiffly.

So it was difficult for him, too? Good! She gathered her purse and locked the door behind them before she settled into the seat beside him in the car. She winced a little, because he hadn't been gentle and it had been her first time.

He cursed under his breath, not missing the hint of discomfort.

"I'm sorry," he said again, his conscience killing him.

She gripped her purse, staring straight ahead. "It's...part of the process, isn't it? Pain?"

"So they say. I wouldn't know. I've never made love to a virgin."

"That wasn't love," she said through her teeth, coloring. "That was a quick roll in the hay, because you had to have a woman and I was handy!"

He cut off the engine and turned to face her, lighting a cigarette with nervous fingers before he opened the window to spare her the passive smoke. "It was quick," he agreed with stung pride. "But not because you were handy and I needed sex. And as I recall, you didn't have the breath to complain when you were screaming under me to satisfy you!"

She buried her face in her hands with anguished shame.

"My God, I didn't mean that," he said wearily, running a hand through his sweaty hair. "I didn't mean to...Tabby, you were incredible. Really, incredible. I wasn't even sure that I'd be able to satisfy you," he said curtly. "You're more woman than I've ever had before."

She couldn't look at him. That made it, somehow, even worse.

"I couldn't manage to draw back, to make an effort to protect you," he said slowly. He looked at her flat stomach and something terrifying leaped into his mind. "Tabby," he said slowly, "tell me that this wasn't a good time to make you pregnant."

She flushed. He looked terrified by the prospect. That registered, even through her anguish. "I don't know," she said miserably. "Oh, Nick . . . !"

She looked vulnerable and very frightened. Probably she was. He cursed under his breath. "That's great," he said icily. "That's just great!"

All her worst nightmares were flowing into the light. She closed her eyes, wished she could go back, wishing she could have a second chance. "You needn't worry that I'll be a nuisance if anything happens," she said through her teeth.

He jerked her around, his face pale. She seemed withdrawn and not quite rational, and fear lanced through him. He hadn't considered her deeply religious outlook.

"We made love, for God's sake!" he burst out. "It's no sin to sleep with someone!"

"Isn't it?" She couldn't look at him. "Then why do I feel ashamed and cheap?"

Her voice had a note that he didn't like. He took her by the shoulders and shook her. "Don't you do anything stupid, do you hear me?" he said angrily.

"I'm not that far gone," she replied tersely. She drew back from him with a long breath. "I want to go back to work, Nick."

He didn't want to leave her like this, but he had no choice. She wouldn't even look at him. He felt alone and uneasy, as if he'd done something unspeakable. He'd never felt like that with another woman in his life. Not that any of his women had ever been innocent.

She wouldn't talk to him. He had to hope she wouldn't go off the deep end. "All right," he said finally. "I'll drive you back." He started the car and drove her to the campus, but he didn't get out when she started to.

"You're through for today?" she asked, with her hand on the door handle, still avoiding his eyes.

"Yes."

She didn't know what to say. She murmured something and scrambled out onto the sidewalk.

Nick watched her go into the building, his eyes dark with worry. He'd fouled up her life and his own with a moment's passion. Now Tabby would avoid him like the plague, and he'd spend the next six weeks worrying himself to death about having accidentally made her pregnant. Why, oh why, hadn't he stayed in Houston and left well enough alone?

Tabby went through the motions of working for the rest of the day, but she felt sick to her stomach. She'd saved up her chastity for twenty-five years to give to the man she loved. Then in a fit of feverish passion, she'd given it to Nick in the middle of a public park.

She groaned out loud and tears stung her eyes. She had to force herself not to cry as she walked down the hall at the end of the day toward the exit. She loved

Nick, but that didn't excuse what she'd let him do. Everything she believed in, everything she'd been taught had gone up in ashes in his arms. She'd wanted him, oh, so much. She hadn't been able to hold back, even when she knew what they were doing was wrong. Why, why, hadn't she tried to stop him?

To make matters worse, Nick didn't call or come over. She felt like something he'd used and thrown aside. He didn't even care enough to see if she was all right, if she'd tried to leap out a window or anything. That was proof that he didn't want her, that he didn't care.

But when the doorbell rang, she flew to answer it, just the same, certain that it was Nick come to apologize.

Instead, it was a contrite, worried Daniel. "I know you're angry at the things I said," he murmured deeply. "I'm sorry. I could see all afternoon how upset you were. I know you and that playboy detective don't have anything going on. I came to apologize."

"Oh, Daniel!" His sympathy and compassion were so unexpected that she threw herself into his arms in the open doorway and cried as if her heart would break.

"There, there," he said uncertainly, backing her into the house while he fumbled the door closed.

Nick had been on his way across the lawn, but neither of them saw him. He'd stopped at the sight of Tabby in a bathrobe throwing herself at the historian.

He stormed back into his own house and slammed the door. He'd felt lower than a snake. He wanted to make sure that Tabby was okay, after fighting his conscience all day. He was sick at his own loss of control. She probably hated him.

He didn't know what he'd been about to say when he spotted her in Daniel's arms. It went right out of his head. Now he was confused and hurt and violently jealous. Was she playing some kind of game? Was she going to take Daniel up to bed and give him the benefit of the experience she'd had with Nick?

And he knew then that Tabby wouldn't do it. Not even if she wanted Daniel to the point of obsession. No, she wasn't that kind of woman.

But she was in the man's arms and apparently happy to be there. How did he equate that with the fervent way she'd given in to him in the park? Did she love Daniel? Was what she felt for Nick only physical after all, and now that she'd satisfied it she didn't want him anymore?

He'd never realized that he had so many insecurities. It had devastated him that he couldn't stop in the park. He'd never lost his head like that, stooping to the seduction of a woman in plain view of anyone who might have walked past. And not just any woman, either, but Tabby, who was virginal. He remembered her soft cry of pain, and then her body had accepted him with such warm sweetness that he'd gone right over the edge. He'd taken her there, too, though. He'd given her heaven. He didn't have to be told to know it. He remembered the things she'd whispered to him, things she probably didn't even recall saying. He remembered the desperate clutch of her hands, the soft, aching moans under his mouth. But most of all, he remembered the heartbreaking way she'd cried when he rolled away from her. She'd been ashamed and hurt, and what he'd said to her afterward hadn't done anything to alleviate the situation between them.

PLAY
SILHOUETTE'S

LUCKY HEARTS

GAME

AND YOU COULD GET

★ FREE BOOKS
★ FREE "KEY TO YOUR HEART" PENDANT NECKLACE
★ FREE SURPRISE GIFT
★ AND MUCH MORE

TURN THE PAGE AND DEAL YOURSELF IN ➡

PLAY "LUCKY HEARTS" AND YOU COULD GET...

★ Exciting Silhouette Desire® novels—FREE
★ "Key to Your Heart" pendant necklace—FREE
★ Surprise mystery gift that will delight you—FREE

THEN CONTINUE YOUR LUCKY STREAK WITH A SWEETHEART OF A DEAL

When you return the postcard on the opposite page, we'll send you the books and gifts you qualify for, absolutely free! Then, you'll get 6 new Silhouette Desire® novels every month, delivered right to your door months before they're available in stores. If you decide to keep them, you'll pay only $2.49* per book—that's a saving of 40¢ off the cover price—plus only 69¢ delivery for the entire shipment!

★ Free Newsletter!

You'll get our subscribers-only newsletter—an insider's look at our most popular authors and their upcoming novels.

★ Special Extras—Free!

When you join the Silhouette Reader Service™, you'll also get additional free gifts from time to time as a token of our appreciation for being a home subscriber.

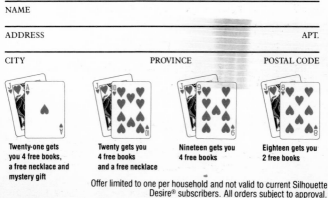

**Business
Reply Mail**

No Postage Stamp
Necessary if Mailed
in Canada

Postage will be paid by

**SILHOUETTE READER SERVICE
PO BOX 609
FORT ERIE, ONT.
L2A 9Z9**

DETACH AND MAIL CARD TODAY

She was probably running to Daniel for comfort, and how could he blame her? He'd given her a moment's pleasure that would be followed by months of shame and anguish and possibly even a child that neither of them wanted.

He didn't know what to do next. His instincts told him to march right over there and bash Daniel's head in with a scotch bottle. The trouble was that first he'd have to empty the scotch bottle.

He picked it up and studied it carefully. Good idea, he thought, nodding. He poured some of it into a glass and drained it. It felt good going down. He sprawled on the sofa and had some more.

About midnight, Nick saw a car leaving Tabby's driveway. It was about time that stuffed shirt went home.

He picked up the phone and punched in Tabby's number. He got two wrong connections. The third time he got Tabby.

"It won't work," he said, carefully enunciating his words. "I am not jealous of Daniel."

"I don't care what you are!" she raged at him. "Go away!"

"Come over and sleep with me," he murmured. "I need you, Tabby."

"I don't need you," she said huskily, her voice thick with tears. "You've been drinking, haven't you?" she asked suddenly as the slur of his deep voice got through her pain.

"Only a bottle or so of whisky," he said reasonably. "Had to empty the bottle. Didn't want to hit him with a full one."

"Hit him?"

"Lover boy," he explained. "I'm going to brain him, Tabby. You tell him to stay away from you. I don't want him touching you. You belong to me."

Her heart raced. But it was only the liquor talking. "No, I don't," she said firmly. "You go away. Leave me alone."

"Can't. Have to—" he hiccuped gently "—solve the case."

"Solve the case then, but you won't get near me again," she said stiffly. "Once was enough."

"No," he murmured. "Not nearly. So sweet, baby. So sweet! Never touched heaven like that before. Only with you, Tabby..."

Flushing, she slammed down the receiver. It rang again, but she ignored it, white-faced, and went to bed.

Never again, she told herself firmly. Oh, no, Nick. Never again.

She pulled the covers over her head and closed her eyes resolutely. She wasn't going to become one of his women. Somehow, someway, she was going to get over him once and for all. If there just weren't any consequences because of her stupidity. She groaned and closed her eyes tighter as she mumbled her prayers. Foremost among them was that she'd have the strength to escape Nick's arms, and that a tiny new life wouldn't be the price of her folly.

Six

Tabby had to force herself to get up and dress and go to work the next morning. She was sick and sore and her mind wasn't on her job. She taught mechanically, but she knew that the emotional turmoil she was experiencing had to show.

It did. Her mirror told her that. She hadn't talked to Nick again since last night. He was probably at home with a humdinger of a hangover, and she didn't care. She was just glad that he wasn't on campus. Having to see him now would make her sick. How could she have forgotten all her principles and given in like that?

Because she loved him, she thought with bitter resignation. To her, it had been a surrender that was a declaration of love and commitment. But to Nick it had been another interlude, a brief moment's pleasure that carried no responsibilities. He hadn't even offered to protect her. She flushed. Actually, she had to admit, he'd been much too involved to have been capable of it. She didn't even know if that was normal behavior for him, or if he'd wanted her too much to think of the consequences or even where they were. It would make it somehow a little more acceptable to think that cool, calm Nick had gone off the deep end because of a monstrous desire for her.

That was hardly likely, though, a man of his sophistication and experience. He'd known exactly how to bring her to ecstasy, and he'd done it. She'd never dreamed that such pleasure even existed. It was probably addictive, she thought miserably, because even with its soreness, her body ached for him all over again. The memories were vivid and sweet, and her skin was ultrasensitive after having known the touch of his hands and mouth.

She agonized over the thought that she'd cut her own throat. Helen had warned her that giving in to him would only chase him away, and that was already happening. If he hadn't been drunk, he'd never have called her at all last night. He wouldn't even respect her now. He'd add her to the rank and file of his conquests, and forget her just as easily as he'd forgotten the others over the years.

Her mind was in limbo. She'd borrowed a small clay tablet, a document from ancient Sumer done in pictographs, to show her class. She'd do well, she thought, to concentrate on what she was getting paid for.

"This tablet dates to the ancient Sumerian civilization," she lectured, displaying it. "So far, now, we've covered the earliest settlement in Mesopotamia, which was located between the Tigris and Euphrates Rivers in what is now southern Iraq. The Sumerians were the first people to develop a written language. Who can tell me the first language they produced?''

A hand went up and she nodded at the dark-haired young man. "Pictographs."

She smiled at him. He was one of her best students, and he had every intention of one day following in her footsteps as an educator. "Very good, Mike," she said. "Pictographic writing, which used symbols to convey language, came first. Then a more sophisticated form of writing called cuneiform, emerged. This used wedge-shaped symbols to represent individual syllables of the language. It was done on a wet clay tablet that was engraved with cuneiform writing using a wedge-shaped reed called a stylus. The tablet was then baked. Thousands of these tablets were found in ancient Sumer.''

"One of them was the Epic of Gilgamesh, wasn't it?" a female student recalled.

"Indeed it was, a series of stories about Gilgamesh, who was a Sumerian king, and his search for immortality. Part of this work involves a certain legend. Does anyone remember which incident in our history it correlates with?"

"The great flood," Mike replied, grinning.

"Yes." She looked at her watch. "That's all the time we have for today. Tomorrow, I'll go over the method of making paper from papyrus reed once more. Don't forget, we have an examination on Wednesday. This one will be an essay examination. If you have problems with any of this material, I'll be in my office this afternoon, or you can make an appointment to see me at a later time.''

She watched them leave and wondered if she'd ever been as young as some of these students. There were a number of older ones, though, some even in their forties and fifties. The days of only young faces on campus were over, and perhaps it was just as well. You were never too old to get a degree, she mused, smiling.

She locked the Sumerian tablet in a glass case to give back to Daniel later, and collected her materials and left the office long enough to go to the rest room. On her way back, she noticed Daniel waiting at her door.

Beside him was a tall, thin young man carrying a camera. Daniel looked faintly irritable. Of course, he always did.

But he smiled at Tabby gently, their quarrel of the day before long forgotten because of the tender way he'd comforted her last night. He'd had no idea why she was upset, thinking it was because he'd argued with her. She hadn't told him, either, or broken their engagement. She would have to, eventually. She couldn't very well marry him when she might be carrying Nick's child. But she couldn't do it yet. She had too much on her mind. All the same, Daniel hadn't asked anything of her, content to just hold her while she cried. She'd made coffee and they'd talked about the book and later, he'd gone home. Nick had seen him leave, she supposed, and been too drunk to remember that he didn't give a damn about her.

It was almost funny, in a way, but she wasn't laughing.

He introduced her to the young man, adding, "Tabitha, do you have that clay tablet from Sumer? This is Tim Mathews. He's with the *Washington Inquirer,* and he'd like to photograph it."

She flushed, more out of having to face Daniel and pretend that nothing had changed, on top of the guilt of what she'd done with Nick, than for any other reason. But the flush made her look self-conscious and nervous.

"Of course! I meant to give it back to you. I'll just unlock my door..."

A shriek came out of the biology lab as they passed it, followed by a demanding voice. "Where have you been? You're going to be boiled one day, don't you know that? How did you do this?"

There was more muttering, something about antiseptic. Tabby didn't listen. She was too nervous.

She fumbled the key into the lock. The door opened very easily. She looked down at a mangled paper clip and absently picked it up, wondering which of her students had untwisted it and left it there.

"It's right through here," she said, leading them into the small library that flanked her even smaller office. She stopped dead.

"Well, what a nice touch this is!" the reporter grinned, hefting his .35 millimeter camera on the broken glass of the case. "You said that a clay tablet was supposed to be in here under lock and key?"

"Yes," Daniel said uncomfortably. He glanced at Tabby. "You're sure you locked the door to this room? It wasn't locked when we came in."

"I'm positive!" she said huskily. "I'm positive I did. Daniel, you have to believe me!"

"The tablet's gone, all right. Look at this. Was there something else in here, a fur pelt, maybe?" He held up a tiny sample of hair.

"I don't remember," Tabby said. She felt sick.

"This looks bad, Tabitha," Daniel said quietly.

"I know that," she murmured miserably and leaned against the wall. "Someone's out to get me."

"It does look that way. Here, I'd better take you up to the dean and let you explain this to him," Daniel said.

"Just a quick shot of you, Dr. Harvey, okay?" the reporter said quickly.

Tabby shielded her face and followed Daniel out into the hall. Her heart was rocketing into her throat. The dean would never believe this. He'd be certain that she'd broken the case and taken the artifact, to make it look like an outside job. She was innocent, but nobody was ever going to believe it now.

"I'm sorry," Daniel was saying. "I'm sorry, too, that we had an argument over Reed. I let him get to me. But this, this accusation of theft . . . I'll never believe it."

"Thank you, Daniel. Honestly, I didn't do it," she told him. "Why is this happening to me?" She broke down and began to cry. Daniel pulled her against him and comforted her as best he could, but she cried as if her heart was broken.

The dean listened quietly to the new development and grimaced. "And there was a reporter in there with you, Myers?" he asked sharply. "That's just wonderful." He threw up his hands. "This is going to be devastating to our reputation!"

"I didn't take it," Tabby said proudly.

"What?" He glanced at her. "Oh. No, of course you didn't, Dr. Harvey. I'm not naive enough to believe you'd risk your job and your reputation by taking two artifacts that would only be of value to a college or a collector."

"Thank you," she said softly. "But nobody else is going to believe me. And the press will have a field day with this, I'm afraid."

"That's true. It isn't going to be pretty."

"What about the trustees?" Daniel asked.

"I don't know. I'll meet with them tonight and we'll see. Go home, Dr. Harvey, and get some rest. We'll talk tomorrow."

She nodded, too tired to argue.

Daniel went out to the parking lot with her, supportive but distant. "The reporter seems to have gone, at least," he murmured. "I really hate this for you, Tabitha."

He didn't know the half of it. In the space of two days, her life had turned over.

She smiled wanly. "I hate it, too."

"Shall I come over again tonight and we can work? Would that help get your mind off your worries?"

"No," she said quickly. She had to break the engagement. What she'd done had made it possible, but she had to find the right way to break it to Daniel. Right now, her mind was in shards.

"I'll see you tomorrow, then," he said easily. "Get some rest, dear."

"Thanks."

She got into the car and drove home. She needed to tell Nick about this new development, but the thought of even talking to him was just unthinkable.

She phoned Helen, instead, on the pretext that she couldn't reach Nick.

"A case was broken into and another artifact is gone," Tabby told her. "Now they'll be sure I did it. The thing was in my office and the door wasn't locked. They'll blame me ... !"

"I'll find Nick and send him right over there," Helen began.

"No! I mean, no, I won't be here. I have to leave for a while. Just…just tell him what I told you, all right?"

"I'll tell him. You're sure…?"

"I'm sure. Thanks."

"No problem. I'll be in touch."

Tabby hung up the telephone. Then she went out and drove her car back to the campus, leaving it in an isolated permitted parking space. She hailed a cab and went home, and she didn't turn the lights on all night. Let Nick wonder where she was. Anything was better than having to face him with the memory of the day before between them. Talking to him on the phone, even when he was drunk, was far less traumatic than having him look at her and see her as she had been—abandoned and totally wanton.

Nick had gotten up with a vicious headache and slept late. It was getting to be an unpleasant habit, and he had to get out of it. The scotch was gone, he noted, and didn't replace it. He had to get a grip on himself. Toward that end, he spent the day searching out leads. He made time to dash into the college and pick up a sample of animal fur that he'd found once more in Tabby's office and take it by the FBI lab. After that, he avoided the college for the rest of the day. He'd seen Tabby briefly, but he'd avoided her and she hadn't seen him. He was no more eager to face Tabby than she apparently was to face him.

He got home that evening to find a message from his sister on his answering machine. He called her, and she relayed Tabby's message.

"She couldn't get me, you say?" He looked out the window, concerned. It disturbed him that Tabby might have gone off the deep end over what they'd done together. But her car wasn't there and the lights were all off. More than likely she was at a motel, he thought furiously, so that she wouldn't have the threat of his company to talk things over. Or maybe she was with Daniel again. Maybe she was at his house tonight, trying to patch up things with him. That made Nick even angrier.

"That's what she said," Helen replied. "She sounded funny. Is she all right, Nick?"

He didn't want to think about how she was. "I'll get back to you," he told her, and hung up.

Later that evening, his old friend from the FBI lab phoned him.

"I've got some news for you about that animal fur. You sitting down?" he asked Nick amusedly.

"I am now. Shoot."

Nick listened and began to smile. Then light bulbs flashed on in his head. Could it be that simple? Tabby was going to be shocked and so were a few other people, if his theory proved true. It was a good thing no blame had been placed and no accusations had been made, or there would be plenty of red faces.

He picked up the telephone and called the dean of the college at home. He asked a few questions and made a request, which was immediately granted. He did not reveal his theory.

Now he knew what to do, and how to go about proving Tabby's innocence. It was a matter of setting a trap and springing it, in just the right way and with just the right people to witness it.

But he needed to talk to Tabby. He picked up the telephone and punched in her number, then waited impatiently. He had to know if she was at home, or if she was with her idiot fiancé.

After he was ready to give up, the receiver was picked up.

"Yes?" Tabby asked quietly.

"It's me," Nick said.

Her heart leaped. She almost put the receiver down. She hadn't spoken to him since he'd called over there drunk.

"Are you still there?" Nick asked irritably.

"Yes. I'm, uh, distracted. Another artifact has disappeared."

"So Helen said," he replied pointedly. "I gather that you can't stand the thought of speaking to me these days? Can't you deal with the situation between us?"

She swallowed and sat down, still holding the telephone. "I . . . don't know how one deals with situations like this," she confessed. "I've never had to before."

"You don't need to remind me that I seduced you," he replied tersely. "I do have a conscience."

She took a very slow breath. "I should have said no."

"That would have been interesting," he said. "Do you think it would have stopped me at that stage?"

She blushed like a tomato. "I don't know . . ."

"For the record, it's very difficult for a man to draw back once he's reached that point. Even though I've never personally been that hot, I've heard about men who have."

He was telling her something, but she was too self-conscious to pursue it. She straightened. "Have you found out anything new?"

"Yes. Don't ask, I won't tell you. I have something planned for tomorrow night that will probably clear you."

"You know who did it?" she asked hesitantly.

"Yes."

"Nick . . . it isn't Daniel?"

"Do you love him?" he asked harshly. "I want an answer," he said when she hesitated. "Right now, Tabby!"

"As you said yourself, if I did, how did I wind up in the grass with you?"

"Sarcasm doesn't suit you," he told her. "I'm sure you've read that lust and love don't always go hand in hand."

"You should know."

"Yes," he said angrily. "I should. But since I've never experienced love, I'm hardly the person to ask for a comparison."

Her eyes closed. He was telling her that all he'd felt was lust. Her stomach flipped over.

His indrawn breath was audible when he realized what he'd said to her. "I care for you," he ground out. "You're part of my life, part of my past. We've been together forever. I wanted you, but it wasn't impersonal lust. If it had been only that, I'd never have lost control so badly that I couldn't protect you from an unwanted pregnancy."

"Unwanted on your part. You've certainly made that very clear," she said stiffly.

"I'm not ready," he groaned. "I'm restless, unsettled. I don't want to have to live in one place yet."

"I haven't asked you to."

"If you are pregnant . . . !"

"If I am pregnant," she said very calmly, "we'll talk about it then. I won't have an abortion, so you can forget that option right now."

He didn't say a word. He didn't know what to say. The thought of a child of his growing up without him was painful. It would be another person to risk losing. His eyes closed in fear. Lucy had loved him, really loved him, and she'd died. He didn't want anybody else to love him and die. Especially, he thought in anguish, someone he loved as well.

Tabby didn't know what he was thinking. She only knew that he was totally silent. She quietly put the receiver down before he spoke. Afterward she didn't know if he'd have said anything else or not. She told herself she didn't care.

She got out her books and prepared her lesson for the next day. Teaching anthropology was challenging. There had to be field trips, and they usually involved some physical labor. Digs had to be measured and roped off, spaded down to the plow zone, and then very carefully excavated with trowels and screens. It was laborious and challenging, but very rewarding.

The study of man was a delight. She'd become obsessed with it in college and had known very quickly that she wanted to teach it when she finished. She'd obtained her bachelor's degree and then gone straight into graduate school to work for her Ph.D. It had been a long climb, and left her no time for a social life. When she wasn't studying, she was attending lectures, going to museums, haunting exhibitions and collections. She lived and breathed anthropology. It was her greatest love, next to Nick. Now she stood to lose it. She hadn't realized how much it meant to her until it was too late.

If only she knew something about detective work! She had to depend on Nick, because he was the only person who could extricate her from this tangled web. But the sooner he did that, the sooner he'd be on a plane back to Houston. She grimaced. She didn't want him to leave, even if it meant bearing the shame and guilt longer. But she had to be realistic. What would he want with her, now that he'd satisfied his curiosity and his hunger.

She put out the light and went to bed. Perhaps things would be brighter after a night's sleep.

Seven

Tabby went through the motions of lecturing until her classes were over, but almost three days after her fall from grace, she felt as if what she'd done in the park was visible to everyone she came in contact with.

Daniel came in just as she finished, his expression faintly apologetic.

"I should never have brought that reporter in. I'm afraid I've made things worse for you," he began slowly.

"It's all right," she said without feeling. "It wasn't your fault, Daniel."

He hesitated, searching for the right words. "Listen, Tabby, we looked at engagement rings, but we never decided on one," he said after a minute. "Suppose we go to a different jeweler..."

It was the very opening she needed, and she took it. Reluctantly, but firmly, she turned to look at him. "I can't marry you, Daniel. I'm very sorry."

He scowled. "Why not?"

"I just . . . can't, that's all." She lowered her head. "It wouldn't be right."

He moved closer. "Tabitha, it can't be because of this theft charge . . . !"

"It isn't. Daniel, we're really not suited," she said miserably. "I'll still help you with your research, you know I will. But marriage is something I can't agree to. Not now."

"You won't mind helping me with the book?"

She felt even sicker that the broken engagement mattered less to him than his precious manuscript. Just as Nick had said, Daniel had probably only been using her. He was a shallow man, in many ways, with no real deep feelings. This was evidence of it.

"I won't mind."

He smiled, rubbing his hands together. "Well, that's fine, then. I'll phone you later."

He started out. Something seemed to occur to him. He turned, his gaze oddly hesitant. "You and Reed. There's something there, isn't there?"

"Not really," she said, lifting her face. "Nick wants no part of a permanent relationship."

He studied her curiously. "I see. Well, no hard feelings about the engagement. I'll phone you tonight about the research notes for that next chapter."

"Yes. Fine."

Before the last syllable died on the air, he was down the hall, whistling happily.

Tabby gathered her papers and walked listlessly down the hall. On the way out, the dean stopped her.

"I'm sorry to tell you this, but the story is all over the papers and the board of trustees feels that a leave of absence is in order, just temporarily," he said stiffly. "There are reporters all over the place. I was going to suggest that you go home after your last class, but I gather that you're doing it already." He cleared his throat, averting his eyes from Tabby's stricken face. "Under the circumstances, I think it would be best to have one of the other anthropologists take your classes for a few days. Until this matter is resolved."

"You don't think I did it?" she asked miserably.

"No," he said. "Try not to worry. It will all work out, you know."

His smile was as limp as her heart. She nodded. "I'll not come in until you notify me, then. I'll avoid the press as well. But I'm not guilty," she added solemnly. "If I meant to steal something, it would be one of the gold pieces from the Troy exhibit or a jeweled brooch from the Spanish galleon collection. A piece of ancient pottery... well, it's hardly dear, is it, except to historians and anthropologists?"

He looked thoughtful. "My dear, I have considered that aspect. Of course, you're right. It would take a collector to appreciate it. But we're under the gun, you see."

"Yes. I see," she said sadly. "I only wish I'd thought to make that point to the reporter."

"I'll make sure that I do," he assured her.

She went on out to her car, hoping that she could reach it before any of the press found her. She'd never felt quite so bad in all her life. Nick had seduced her, she might be pregnant, and now she was in danger of losing her job. It was enough to make a saint cry.

Tabby was no saint, and cry she did, all the long way home. She was still bawling when she drove up at her own door. For a long time, she let the healing tears roll down her face. When she was finally drained of emotion, she wiped her red eyes and blew her equally red nose and got out of the car.

Nick, meanwhile, was still uncovering leads. Though he had a theory as to the identity of the culprit, he had to keep an open mind. He'd had Helen do some checking on Dr. Day and she discovered that his wife had inherited a small fortune from a deceased relative. That would explain the Lamborghini. Dr. Flannery, on the other hand, was in financial difficulties *because* of *his wife.* She'd just left him for another man, and the skip tracers said that the gossips were having a field day speculating about his relief. His wife had been much younger and not terribly faithful, either. Flannery was hardly heartbroken.

That left Daniel. His falsification of past records still put him at the top of the list of suspects. But why would he take an ancient artifact? It wasn't even from the period he and Tabby were working on. And no background check of his past came up with a record of theft. Only that radical stage.

While he was ruling out suspects, the telephone rang. It was one of the local police officers whom Nick had contacted, and he set up a time and place for a stakeout at the college. He made one other telephone call and talked to another potential witness. So much for witnesses. Now he had to bait and set the trap.

Hopefully Tabby would soon be out from under suspicion. He could go away and let her get her life back together. He put his head in his hands and groaned. God, if only he'd never touched her! Guilt was eating him alive. Sweet, gentle Tabby had never hurt a soul in her life. Her only weakness was him, had always been him. He'd taken what she'd offered, but it gave him no pleasure to remember that most of the enjoyment had been his. She'd barely had anything, even at the last. He hadn't given her even a sweet memory of his lovemaking to carry down the years. He should have waited. It should have been a different place, with all the time in the world to teach her what lovemaking was. He should have been kinder to her. Cursing, he got up and went back to his notes.

His theory was right on the money, especially now that he had the missing evidence. He needed to make a move, but he had to tell Tabby what he was going to do. That wasn't going to be easy. He was asking her to trust him with her academic future. Perhaps she wouldn't want to.

He went to his window to see if Tabby was home. Sure enough, her car was in the driveway tonight.

But he hesitated about going over there. What he'd found out would offer her some consolation, but his headlong rush into intimacy and the aftermath still had him upset. It had devastated Tabby. He hated the memory of how she'd looked afterward. Her puritan ideals were in hell. He knew what a little saint Tabby was. He'd done something unforgivable to her, really messed up her life. Even if she didn't become pregnant, the way they'd made love would haunt her forever.

He knew he'd treated her shabbily, making love to her in the park that way, but he hadn't meant to insult her. He'd wanted her so desperately that he simply lost control. Years of denied hunger had overwhelmed him—and certainly her as well. But he was experienced enough to call a halt, and he hadn't. He hadn't even managed to protect her.

He wasn't certain if it would be kinder to go and talk to her or stay away.

Finally he decided that staying away, giving her more time to get over her rawness at what had happened, might be the best course of action. But this night, like the previous ones, wasn't pleasant. His conscience and fear that he might have accidentally made her pregnant gave him such fits that he wound up watching all-night movies just to keep his mind off it.

Tabby, meanwhile, had too much time on her hands and she hated the sight of herself in a mirror. The fact that she couldn't go to work and stay busy made it worse. She spent the day cleaning house and letting her answering machine take care of the incoming calls. Most of them were from the press, and she was glad that she hadn't seen a morning paper. Probably it bore a headline that included her.

One call late in the day attracted her attention, because it was from Helen Reed.

She picked up the receiver with shaking hands. "Helen! Am I glad to hear your voice! The phone's gone off the hook all day, and the dean won't let me work...!"

"What is going on out there?" Helen interrupted. "You're in the papers, did you know? It's all here, about the missing artifact and an accusation against you, that you've been temporarily suspended. So that was what that call was all about the other day, wasn't it? Tabby, I know you don't steal things!"

"Well, no," Tabby said. She sank onto the couch, her heart beating wildly. "It's in all the papers, I suppose? Wire services, too?" She groaned. "Oh, Helen, what am I going to do?"

"Nick's there, isn't he? He's supposed to be solving the case."

"Yes, Nick's around," Tabby said stiffly. Her eyes closed on a wave of sick shame. "He doesn't even have any suspects."

"But he does. Well, only one, really. Dr. Flannery and Dr. Day checked out okay, but your friend Daniel Myers didn't."

"Daniel?"

"I'm afraid so. There's him and some new theory that Nick won't trust me with yet."

"What did you find out about Daniel?"

"Sorry, pet, but that's confidential. Don't you worry, I know Nick's got enough to clear you right now."

"Daniel wouldn't steal an artifact, I don't care what's in his past," Tabby said. "You know him like I do. He's Mr. Straight—the kind of man who lives and breathes law and order. He won't even keep a nickel he finds on the street unless he can't find the person who lost it! Does that sound like a thief?"

Helen hesitated. Nick had said that Tabby didn't care about Daniel, but she didn't sound very uncaring. "No, of course it doesn't," she agreed. "But he was the last suspect left . . ."

"No. There's another one. There's me." Tabby's lips stiffened. "Maybe I walk in my sleep and steal things. Maybe I'm really the culprit only I don't remember. Maybe I have multiple personalities . . . !"

"Tabby, do stop it," Helen said gently. "I know you're upset. But you have to keep your head. It will blow over. Nick will prove your innocence. Honest, he will."

"Pigs will fly," Tabby said wearily. "I have to go. I think a reporter is taking photographs through my window."

"Throw a pot at him."

Tabby laughed hysterically. "Then I'd accidentally kill him and go to prison for murder. That's the way my luck's running."

"You're just hopeless."

"You don't know the half of it."

"Try to get a good night's sleep, won't you? If you see Nick, have him call me. I may have something else in a couple of hours."

"If I see him." *I hope I don't,* she added silently. "Thanks for calling."

"Call me if you need me, will you?" Helen asked impatiently. "And don't worry. I promise you, everything will be all right."

"The truth will out, in other words?" She laughed cynically. "Yes, but sometimes that takes twenty years. I'll be forty-five."

"Go to bed."

"Okay. Good night."

"Yes. You, too."

She put the receiver down. No sooner was it in the cradle than it started ringing again. More reporters. More questions. If she'd been more lucid, she might have given them a statement. But she felt too miserable to even try. There apparently had been a man with a camera at the window, because her flower bed had footprints in it. Great, she thought. Now they had a picture to print. She closed the curtains, as she should have done much earlier, and turned on the television to drown out her worries.

Her conscience tormented her for the next two days. She didn't look toward Nick's house. She talked to Daniel on the telephone, having discouraged him from coming over. A reporter was camped on her front porch, making coffee on a hot plate using stolen current from her outside electrical outlet. She wondered if she could call a rival paper and make news out of that? It was really amazing that a small stolen artifact could make this much press. It must be a slow week for news. . . .

There was a knock on the door at the end of the third day. She peered out at Nick and reluctantly opened the door.

"I ran off your happy camper," he remarked, nodding to where the reporter had been sitting. "Unplugged his hot plate. He's afraid of starvation without his coffeepot, so he's gone to a local waffle house to get a cup."

"Thank you."

"Are you going to let me in?" he asked, lounging carelessly against the door frame. He looked nonchalant, which was the last thing he actually was. He felt nervous and vaguely ashamed, emotions he'd been gloriously unfamiliar with before.

"I suppose so." She opened the door and he came inside. She was wearing a lightweight blue denim shirtwaist dress, with her hair in a long braid down her back. No makeup, no fussy hairdo. She looked a little plain and Nick felt worse than ever when he saw the dark circles under her eyes and the drawn, pale look about her.

"I gather you've been avoiding me?" he asked.

"You gather right," she replied tersely. "Why did you need to see me, Nick?"

He had to gather his wits again. Her straightforward attack had thrown him. "I've found something," he said quietly. "The thief left a little evidence this time. A tuft of hair and a speck of blood."

"Is the thief a wounded bald man?" she asked.

"Not quite. I took a sample of it over to the FBI lab, had a friend of mine run an analysis of it and I got the results. I haven't even told Helen yet, but I've phoned the police, and I've talked with that reporter who's had you staked out. I've asked them both to come to the college tonight. I want you along as well. We're going to lock ourselves in your office and wait for the thief to strike again. We're even providing some very tempting bait."

Tabby found it difficult to talk to him. She folded her arms across her breasts defensively. "Helen said Daniel is at the top of your list of suspects."

"The last she knew, he was the only one left," Nick replied. His dark eyes narrowed. "That bothers you?"

"Even though we aren't engaged anymore, Daniel is still a colleague and a friend. Yes, it bothers me."

His eyebrows collided. "What do you mean, you're not engaged anymore?"

"I couldn't go through with it. Not after... what happened."

He let out an angry breath and rammed his hands deep into his slacks pockets. "It was just an interlude! Women have them all the time!"

"I don't," she said levelly, meeting his eyes. "And feeling the way I do about it, I can't go to one man when I've been intimately involved with another. Especially now, before I know…"

His eyes fell blankly to her stomach and his teeth clenched. "It doesn't always happen the first time," he said. "There may not be anything to worry about."

"When do you want to go to the college?" she asked, changing the subject.

He couldn't fathom her. His temper was getting out of bounds. He didn't like the way he felt. His eyes slid over her with new knowledge. He knew what she felt like under that concealing dress. He knew the sounds she made in passion and the silky softness of her body as it grew feverish under his… Thoughts and memories like that would never do, he told himself.

"You can ride in with me tonight," he said.

"No, thank you. I'll go with Daniel."

His eyes flashed. "He wasn't invited."

"Nevertheless, he'll be there. You've made him a suspect. I won't tell him that, but I think he's entitled to share in the solving of the mystery."

"We might as well invite the neighbors, too," he grumbled.

"Fine by me. The more people who think I'm innocent, the better. God knows, I'm probably as notorious as Mata Hari by now." She frowned. "Do you suppose anyone thinks I'm really a secret agent stealing ancient microfilm?"

"Hidden inside five-thousand-year-old artifacts," Nick said, shaking his head. "Only one of those grocery store tabloids would buy that."

"Great idea. Where did you say that reporter went?"

"I'll leave you to it," he murmured, refusing to be drawn in. "We'll meet in your office at six."

"Daniel would never take anything that wasn't his," she said as he paused in the open doorway.

He turned and looked at her. "Any more than you would," he agreed. "Don't worry. It isn't Daniel." He studied her wan face for a long time. "It should have been him, in the park, shouldn't it?" he asked bitterly.

Her composed face showed no emotion. "What difference does it make now?"

He let out a long breath. "None, I suppose. For what it's worth, I'd give anything to take it back."

"So would I," she replied miserably.

He made an oddly jerky gesture and went out without looking at her again.

Tabby took a bath and dressed in a becoming purple silk pantsuit to sit and wait for the thief to show up. It was going to be a time fraught with tension with a policeman and a reporter, and with Daniel and Nick in the same room. Probably there would be a free-for-all before the night was over. Good copy for the press, she thought hysterically, and had to choke back laughter.

Her good name would hopefully be cleared. Nick would go back to Houston. She could go back to work and wait out the days until she knew whether or not there would be consequences from the fiery encounter in the park. And afterward, none of it would matter. Except that she could never marry Daniel or anyone else. Despite it all, she loved Nick more than her own life.

It must have been a curse, she thought, placed on her at birth that she'd fall in love with a hopeless bachelor and never get over him.

She phoned Daniel to tell him what was going on, without mentioning that he'd been even briefly a suspect.

"Reed's caught the culprit?" he asked.

"It seems so," Tabby replied. "I really don't think he'd have the police and the press along unless he was reasonably sure that he could prove his allegations, do you?"

"It wouldn't be intelligent. Not," he added, "that I think police work requires intelligence. It seems to me that very few people in detective circles are highly educated."

"You might be surprised."

"Not by your childhood friend," Daniel said. "How are you coming with the new notes I gave you? Have you incorporated them into the book?"

"Yes. I have had little else to do for the past few days, so I've concentrated on it."

"Good girl! Uh, would you mind bringing it with you when you come tonight?"

So much for her thought that he'd pick her up and drive in with her.

"Yes," she told him. "I'll bring it."

"Thanks. See you there at six, then."

He hung up, leaving her holding the receiver with a dial tone on the other end of the line. She seemed fated to get herself involved with men who found her useful but not lovable. She was never going to marry.

But there might be a baby. The thought cheered her, softened her mood. She touched her stomach and allowed herself to dream about what it would be like to hold a tiny human being in her arms.

She'd protect and love it, raise it all by herself. Nick didn't need to offer her support or act as if it were a burden on him. She might not even tell him.

Sure. Great idea, she thought silently. I won't tell him and then I'll spend years hiding the child from Helen every time she comes to visit.

She wasn't being sensible. She picked up her light-weight silk jacket and went out the door.

Minutes later, she unlocked her office. She was early, as she'd needed to be so that she could let the others in. The campus was growing dark, and it was a good thing that no night school classes were held on this floor, or there would have been no use in trying to stake it out.

She put her purse on the desk and sat down. Looking around her, she wondered at the speed of events. Only a short time ago, she'd been engaged to Daniel, working on a book, teaching her classes and going from day to day. She hadn't given Nick a great deal of thought, because after the New Year's Eve party she was certain she'd lost him for good. She'd resigned herself to being Daniel's wife, to teaching classes until she was old enough to retire.

What a joke fate had played on her.

Daniel might take her back, but she couldn't let him without telling him everything that had happened with Nick. That would be unbearable, to have anyone know, much less Daniel, that she'd behaved like some kept woman.

She heard a sound at the door and swung around as two deep voices merged. There was a knock.

"Come in," she called, nervous now.

A uniformed police officer came in with Nick, and a tall young man.

"This is Officer Jennings," Nick introduced the policeman, "and Tim Mathews. Tim has been living on your front porch," he added, "but he's found new quarters. Starting now, he's going to live in your office, instead, and I notice that he's brought his coffeepot with him."

"We've met," Tabby murmured, trying not to laugh.

"Did you know that Tabitha's an anthropologist?"

"Yes. It's interesting, but I'd never be able to be one." Mathews grinned. "I'm not sure I could spell it."

"We're like ancient detectives," Tabby told him. "We dig up mysteries from the past and try to solve them."

"I do the same in the present," Mathews said. "Sorry I had to give you the hard sell, but news is sacred to me."

"Invasion of privacy isn't," she guessed.

He chuckled. "Sorry. No."

"Tell that to a lawyer," Officer Jennings said with a smile.

"We might as well get comfortable," Nick said. He frowned at Tabby. "I thought you said your ex-intended was coming."

"He'll be along," she said.

"It had better be soon, or he'll blow my stakeout."

"Blow what steak out?" Daniel asked as he peered around the door. "Am I late?"

"Yes, but don't let that concern you," Nick said darkly.

"Oh, don't worry, I won't," Daniel said imperturbably. "Do you want this locked?" he asked as he closed the door.

"Please," Nick agreed.

"Did you bring the information I wanted?" Daniel asked Tabby.

"I'm sorry," she said quickly. "I left it on the table by the door."

"Oh, bother," Daniel grumbled. "Well, I'll stop by later. I need those notes."

"She had other things on her mind," Nick said in her defense. "I'm sure you agree that clearing her name is more important than a few notes."

Daniel cleared his throat. "Well, certainly..."

"Have a seat," Nick invited. He settled back into an easy chair, with the reporter perched beside Tabby on a straight-backed chair and Daniel taking up a place by the closet door.

"Isn't this entrapment?" Daniel asked the policeman.

Officer Jennings cocked an eyebrow. "I wouldn't say so. Mr. Reed would know more about that than I would."

"Because he worked for the FBI, I gather," Daniel said irritably.

Jennings shook his head. "Why, no. Because he's the one with the law degree."

Daniel studied the blond man with new interest. "You never said you had a law degree," he murmured. "From what school?"

"Harvard," Nick said with magnificent disdain.

"Oh." Daniel was at a loss for words. He glanced toward Tabby. "You do look washed-out, Tabitha. You need a rest."

"I couldn't agree more," she said, closing her eyes. "It's been the longest week of my life."

"Don't worry, dear girl, we'll clear your name," Daniel said, smiling. "Then you might reconsider that ring I offered you."

She didn't answer. She smiled, her eyes still closed, so that she missed the flash of anger on Nick's face.

"Better settle down and be quiet," Officer Jennings said. "We may be in for a long evening."

"I hope not," Tabby sighed. "I want it to be over."

"Don't we all," Daniel murmured, but no one heard him.

Eight

An hour went by, and then another, with nothing happening. The men began to fidget, and Tabby's heartbeat ran wild. What if Nick was wrong? If no thief appeared, her career would be over.

"This is absurd," Daniel grumbled. "We're wasting time!"

"You're welcome to leave, Dr. Myers," Nick said carelessly. "We'll sweat it out without you."

Daniel looked around and grimaced. "Well, I suppose I could wait a little longer," he added when he saw Tabby's unease.

He settled back, his long legs crossed. Nick stared at Tabby, trying to balance his rocking emotions while he discovered that going back to Houston was less appealing than ever before.

A noise at the door made everyone sit up. Nick put a finger to his lips and eased back into the shadows as the others did.

The door was locked, but someone was working the lock. The noise was loud in the silence, and there was another noise with it, an odd one that was more a grunt.

A minute later, the door opened. It was too dark to see anything. A chair was bumped, and there was a thud, and then the tinkle of glass as a container on Tabby's desk was knocked over.

"Now!" Nick said.

He turned on the lights and the .35 millimeter camera flashed. And everyone stared breathlessly at the image the camera had captured.

There, on the desk, clutching a small cheap plaster statuette that Tabby had put out as bait, was a small hairy biped. Pal, the primate, with a bandage on one hand.

"My God!" Daniel exclaimed. "It's the bloody monkey!"

"Pal!" Tabby gasped. "But he picked the lock, did you see?"

"Yes. And odds are that he's taken his ill-gotten gains to the biology lab and stashed them. Let's go."

They left Pal in the room and followed Nick down the hall to the biology lab. A thorough search of the premises revealed the two missing artifacts and several other more modern things in a large jar that Flannery used to keep large grass plumes in.

"The lipstick I couldn't find," Tabby laughed, picking it up. "My mirror. I thought it had fallen out of my purse. Daniel, here's the pipe stem you thought you lost." She handed it to him.

"What a story this is going to make," Tim chuckled as he snapped photos of the group.

"Shall we take up a collection for Dr. Flannery?" Daniel mused. "He's going to faint when he hears about this. And if the dean doesn't cancel his research grant, I'm a monkey myself."

"You'll make sure the story gets to the wire services, won't you, so that Tabby's cleared?" Nick asked.

"Oh, sure," Tim told them. "She's the best part of the story. Pretty teacher victimized by intelligent ape. I can see the headlines now. We'll have him in love with her and taking personal objects as love tokens."

"Oh, my God," Tabby groaned.

"Now, now, Doc, don't take it like that. How about giving us a quote? That way," he added with an irrepressible grin, "I won't have to set up camp on your front porch again."

"Anything but that! Yes, I'll give you a quote!"

"His hand is bandaged," Nick pointed out. "That was what cinched the case. There was a tiny bit of blood on the fur I found on Tabby's desk. I took the fur to the lab at the FBI building, and the lab tech identified them as primate fur and blood. In fact," he added with an amused look at the reporter, "he gave me the size, weight and approximate age of the monkey. All from that one sample."

"Amazing, isn't it, what they can do?" Mathews agreed. "I watched a program on public TV about those lab detectives. They're really something, especially now with the DNA matching."

"A lot of that still isn't admissible in court," Nick said quietly. "But it will come. Eventually a perpetrator who commits a crime won't have a legal leg to stand on if there's a DNA match."

"Don't you believe it," Mathews replied cynically. "There'll be a way to get around it, right up to copping a sample of an innocent man's blood and leaving it at the scene."

"You reporters," Nick began irritably.

"Don't blame me," Mathews returned, placing a hand on his heart. "I would not for all the world shatter your illusions, sir, but mankind is rotten to the core for the most part."

"Not all of it," Tabby broke in. "There are some good people."

"You have to dig pretty hard to find them, though. If you'll give me that quote, Doc, I'll get out of your hair."

Tabby gave him one, hoping it would be the end of the oddest chapter in the history of her life. Pal's unmasking was enough to take her mind off her own problems, for a while at least. She was grateful for that.

"I'll drop by in the morning and get those notes," Daniel told Tabby, "on my way to school. I, uh, could give you a lift if you want me to."

Tabby smiled. "Thanks, Daniel."

He smiled back. "I'm glad you were cleared." He glanced toward Nick, who was talking to the reporter and Officer Jennings. "I thought for a while there I might be a suspect. You know, back in the early seventies, I marched in an antiwar rally. I didn't put that on my record for fear that they might think me a radical."

"Nothing would be less likely than that," Tabby told him. "And maybe you weren't a suspect," she hedged to spare his feelings.

"All the same, isn't it a good thing this is over?"

"Yes. A good thing." Because it meant that Nick would go back to Houston and she could pick up the threads of her own life. What a dismal fate, she thought silently.

Nick walked her out to her car after the reporter and the policeman had gone. Daniel was locking up after them.

"You could ride home with me," he suggested. "Daniel can bring you back in the morning to pick up your car. I heard him suggest giving you a lift," he added when she frowned.

"I don't think..."

"Good. Don't." He steered her toward his own car, his jaw firmly set. "It's late and this isn't a safe city at night. I'll feel better if you're with me."

What in the world made him think she was safe with him, after the ease with which he'd seduced her? she thought hysterically. But she didn't say it.

They rode home in a tense silence. Nick didn't pull into her driveway when they reached the neighborhood. He parked the car in his own driveway. It didn't alarm Tabby at first. Not until he locked the car and pulled her along with him toward his front door.

"I won't go in there with you," she said stubbornly.

"Yes, you will," he replied quietly, his dark eyes holding hers as he inserted his key into the lock and opened the door. "We have some serious talking to do."

"We can talk tomorrow...!"

"I'm leaving in the morning."

"Oh."

She went with him, her head bent down, feeling empty and forlorn and totally vulnerable.

"Sit down." He motioned her to the sofa. He took off his jacket and his tie, unbuttoning the top buttons of his shirt. "Will you have something to drink?"

"No. Thank you."

"I mean coffee," he said defensively.

"Oh. Well . . . Yes, then."

He put the drip coffeemaker on and then came back to sit across from her in an armchair. "Don't look so shattered, Tabby," he said gently. "You've been completely cleared. I'm sure the dean will have his apologies ready in the morning." He smiled faintly. "Along with Dr. Flannery."

"It wasn't really Dr. Flannery's fault. I feel guilty that you had to pry into my colleagues' pasts to clear me, when it wasn't really necessary."

"We didn't know it wasn't necessary. Besides, I haven't told you what I found out. I won't tell anyone else, either," he said curtly. "I'm a private detective. The operative word is 'private.'"

"I know that. But I seem to have made a lot of trouble for everyone," she confided.

He studied her quietly, wondering at how easily she fit into his private life, how she seemed to belong. He was being fanciful, he told himself. He had no intention of marrying her. He wanted her to understand that.

He clasped his hands together between his knees. "I wanted to apologize, again, for what happened. And to tell you that if there are . . . complications . . . I want to be told."

"I'll tell you. But there's no need, because I'm not going to get rid of a child just to suit you, Nick, no matter how inconvenient he might be."

He cursed sharply and vividly. "I haven't said...!"

She stood up. "You needn't say anything." Her face colored as she stared at him, remembering how his body had felt against hers.

"You can't handle it, can you, Tabby?" he asked quietly. "Having sex with me is some kind of mortal sin. I suppose having it happen spontaneously and almost publicly like that is what hurts the most."

"Nick..."

He moved close and took her by the shoulders. "You're incredibly naive for a woman your age," he said. He searched her eyes. "And what I hate most is that I didn't even take the time to teach you all the pleasures of lovemaking."

"Please, don't," she said huskily.

"Just this, darling," he said softly, his eyes dropping to her mouth. He felt an anguish of desire as his head bent. "Just a few kisses, little one..." he breathed into her mouth.

He kissed her deeply, his arms bending her body up into the hard curve of his, holding her gently but firmly. She struggled at first, but the need to experience him again was betraying her will.

His lean hands slid down her back to her hips and tugged rhythmically, moving her against the growing arousal of his body.

She caught her breath and he felt it in her kiss. His mouth opened, his tongue probing deeply, insistently. She gave in to him and began to make odd, high-pitched little noises. She relaxed, letting him deepen the intimacy of the embrace. Her hands caught at his shirt and clung.

His head spun. She was his. She couldn't resist him any more than he could resist her.

"You're sweet, Tabby," he whispered. "You're sweeter than honey."

She was breathing unsteadily already. His hands slid around her and up to cup her breasts, caress them into hard passion. She felt him unfastening hooks and buttons, but all she could think of was how to get closer to him. She loved him. Nothing else seemed to matter, not even the fear and uncertainty in the back of her mind.

He touched bare, warm, soft skin, and she arched back. His mouth found her, caressed her, made her shiver with her need.

It was too late to draw back. He knew it almost at once, and when he looked into her misty, half-closed eyes, he knew that she needed him as much as he needed her. He was helpless against his desire for her.

This, then, was passion, Tabby thought dizzily as he picked her up and carried her upstairs. This helpless surrender that heard no reason, knew no resistance, was what kept women and men bound together despite their differences. She wanted him as she'd never dreamed she could, despite the trauma of their first time. She loved him so! And this would be the last time...

She heard a door open, heard it close. She felt the bedspread under her bare back, felt his hands removing fabric, caressing, seducing.

He was whispering to her, things that made her body burn, her mind sing. She felt him touching her in all the ways he'd touched her in the park. Except that this time, he held back. He aroused her to fever pitch and then pulled her gently to him, and held her, shivering, until she calmed. Then he began all over again, light caresses, light touches, his lips on her body, his mouth suckling hungrily at her breasts while his hands teased her into a state of insane desire.

The lights were out. For an instant she was sorry, because she wanted to see it, to see him, to watch as they blended into one human being in their feverish rush toward intimacy.

But there wasn't enough light to make out his face as he came over her, into her, and she clutched at his hips, crying out as he eased completely down into stark possession.

He poised there, barely breathing, feeling her in every cell of his body. She moved, crying out, pleading, but his lean hand stilled her hips.

"No," he choked. "No. Lie still."

"Please!"

"Trust me," he whispered shakily. "Tabby, lie still and let me...calm down. I want it to last all night, sweetheart," he said into her open mouth. "I want to take you up and bring you down until you can't bear it, and then I want to explode with you into a thousand lights. Help me, little one. Lie still. Yes. Still."

He calmed her. She cried helplessly, but she obeyed. She felt the tension drain out of him. Then he began yet again, his mouth tracing, touching, cherishing, his hands teasing her back into ecstasy. He didn't move, or lift, and she could feel the depth of his possession, the strength and power of it growing by the second. She grew frightened of its power and whispered it involuntarily.

"Shh," he whispered softly. "You're safe. I won't hurt you. I'll never...hurt you...baby!"

He began to move, ever so tenderly, his body a caress in itself as he kissed her and rocked above her in a rhythm that carried her up and over the edge, long before he was ready.

He felt her convulse and begin to cry, great tearing bursts of sound that mirrored the anguished completion he gave to her. He hadn't wanted to bring it this quickly, because he wasn't ready. But it was all right. She was capable of endless satisfaction. He smiled as he let her rest for a few seconds, turned away for a moment, and then began to arouse her again.

It was a long, long time later when his movements became rough and powerful and urgent. She heard the tenor of his breathing change, felt his body coil and begin to vibrate with its terrible tension. When the pleasure took him, he lifted almost completely off the bed, and she saw his head go back as she felt and heard him experience ecstasy.

He cried out her name in throbbing gasps, his body shuddering so violently that she was almost afraid for him. Then he finally pulled slowly away from her and fell onto his back, and the convulsions were still there, only worse.

"At least," he whispered when he stopped shaking, "this time I managed to protect you."

She only dimly realized what he'd done, what he meant. But she was too tired to analyze it. She closed her eyes and slept, exhausted and drained from pleasure.

When she awoke, it was to light coming in the windows. It took several seconds before she realized where she was. She sat up, feeling sore and uneasy, the sheet falling to her bare breasts. She was nude, and very uncomfortable. She realized why at the same time Nick came out of the bathroom with a towel around his hips.

He paused beside the bed, and he didn't smile. His dark eyes went to her breasts and lingered there.

She couldn't manage to pull the sheet back up. Just looking at him made her sing inside. Her eyes went down his perfectly made body, over his hairy chest to his flat, muscular stomach where the towel caught.

"Want to see all of me?" he asked quietly. "I don't mind." And he dropped the towel.

He was beautiful. She'd never seen a sculpture as perfect as he was, and her eyes told him so.

"You're just as devastating to me, Tabby," he replied. He bent down and pulled the sheet away, revealing the body he'd possessed so thoroughly. He loved looking at her. She was every dream he'd ever dreamed.

As he looked, his body reacted. He chuckled ruefully at the instant effect she had on him, and she blushed.

"I suppose you're on the verge of being the walking wounded this morning?" he asked with resignation.

She blushed more. "If you mean, am I sore... Yes."

He nodded. "That's what I meant, little one." He sighed. "Just as well, I suppose. Last night I was able to protect you, but I have nothing but my willpower this morning. At least we had last night. I didn't want to leave without showing you what it should have been like that day in the park."

"Well, you did," she said, sitting up, tugging the sheet around her as the shame came back again, harder. "You showed me very graphically. Thank you for the lesson."

He retrieved his towel and wrapped it around his lean hips, taking longer than he needed to as he tried to manage the right words. "It wasn't a lesson. It was an apology."

"You're very expert," she said lightly. "Maybe one day I'll be able to appreciate that properly."

"You're unworldly," he replied, frowning. "But you'll learn about the real world, outside that shell you've been living in. It's not such a bad world, Tabby. Men and women make love all the time without guilt or consequences . . ."

She looked at him, and he colored. "I have to go now. I have classes to teach."

He shouldn't feel ashamed, he told himself. He had no reason to feel that way! He went back into the bathroom and slammed the door. When he came out again, freshly shaven, Tabby was back in her silk suit and her hair was in its bun. Except for makeup, she looked just as she had before. Almost. There was a new sadness in her eyes, a new knowledge, a shamed lack of innocence.

"Damn it, you wanted me!" he raged. "You wanted me!"

She turned and looked at him, unblinking. "I loved you," she said simply. "I don't think I'm telling you anything you didn't already know. I wanted you because of the way I feel about you. If you loved me back, I don't think I could be ashamed of what we did. But you don't," she said, almost accusingly. "You need me, physically, but I'm just another conquest to you, another casual lover. That's what makes it so...sordid.''

He was lost for words. Actually lost for them. Tabby had been part of his life forever. Now he was likely to lose her, because he'd precipitated a relationship neither of them was ready for. He might have wished it undone, but his body throbbed with feverish ecstasy at the delight hers had given him even now. He ached to have her again, and again, and again...

If he'd ever wondered before, he knew now that Tabby loved him. It had felt like love, when she wrapped herself around him and gave him such pleasure that he'd all but lost consciousness from it. Love. A child. Perhaps a son. A little boy. His eyes kindled as he considered for the first time in his life the possibility of creation that day in the park.

Tabby didn't see the smile, much less guess what he was thinking. She went toward the closed bedroom door and opened it. She had to go home in broad daylight and the whole neighborhood would probably see her. But it didn't seem to matter anymore if her reputation was ruined. She didn't deserve to have one anyway, having behaved with the abandon of a loose woman. She was Nick's lover now, not the prim and upright young lady she'd been before he came back to Washington.

"Tabby, don't go yet," he said. "I want to talk."

"Well, I don't," she said, and she didn't look back. She was breaking up inside, but she wasn't going to let him know that. She loved him, but he felt no such emotion for her. It was best not to rake over the ashes.

He cursed roundly and tried to go after her, but she was in her house and gone. He slammed back into his house.

He'd wanted to explain his changing feelings to Tabby, but she wasn't in any mood to listen to him. He'd only planned to kiss her a little, make light love to her. But, just like the last time, he'd lost control completely the moment he touched her. He smiled ruefully at his own vulnerability, and reflected that if Tabby had had any real experience of men, she'd have known that he was as helpless as she was. A man didn't lose control with a woman unless there were powerful emotions at work. But Tabby didn't know that. And she wouldn't stand still long enough to let him tell her.

Well, he'd start working on her. Now that he knew he was capable of commitment, he had to convince her that his playboy days were behind him. At least, he'd cleared her name. That was going to take some of the pressure off her and make her more rational.

After taking a cab to work Tabby lectured her class on the techniques of uncovering a midden—a layer of cultural artifacts—touching on new legislation that required respect for human remains and their reinterment.

"This is a good thing," she commented as she sat on the edge of her desk, watching her students. "For too long, certain members of our profession have paid too little attention to the human dignity we owe those who came before us. Bones have been pushed into boxes or into drawers at museums and universities with no respect for the people they once were. This is changing, and it should."

"I certainly wouldn't want anyone to dig up my great-grandmother and keep her bones in a box at a museum," one student remarked.

"Nor would I," Tabby replied.

Class let out and Tabby had a lonely lunch at the canteen until Daniel came up, rubbing his hands together and sat down beside her with a cup of coffee.

"I've just had a telephone call from the publisher I sent that proposal to," he told her. "They're interested!"

She brightened. "Daniel, that's wonderful!"

"Suppose I come over tonight and we work up the outline for the last three chapters?"

She hesitated because all day she'd felt guilty that she hadn't let Nick talk to her when he'd wanted to. She felt weak and disgusted with herself for the ease of her surrender, but he hadn't acted as if it were some casual interlude. He'd been...different. Perhaps there was a reason for it, but she hadn't let him speak. She wanted to. She had to know if there was any possibility of a future for the two of them.

On the other hand, it wouldn't do to sit home all by herself and wait for him to come around.

"All right," she told Daniel. "I'll look for you around five. I'll make a light supper for us."

"Just like old times," he said, smiling. "Fine, darling."

She finished her day's work, feeling so good as members of the faculty congratulated her on being cleared. So did Dr. Flannery, but he looked distinctly uncomfortable.

"They're going to discontinue my program," he said miserably. "And Pal is going back to the zoo. I suppose I'll do as well studying iguanas, though," he said, brightening. "They're delivering a lovely five-foot specimen next week!"

Iguanas, she recalled, looked like prehistoric reptiles. Five feet? "Do they bite?" she asked nervously.

"They're vegetarians, Dr. Harvey," he said, grinning. "Besides—" he leaned close, looking around them "—he won't be able to pick locks!"

He laughed, and so did she.

Late that afternoon, she took a perfect quiche out of the oven and put it and the green salad she'd made on the table while Daniel poured coffee. They had a quiet meal, like old times, and then sprawled in the living room to work on the manuscript. Daniel took off his jacket and tie and shoes, as he usually did, and unbuttoned the top button of his shirt. Tabby, in yellow shorts and a tank top, with her hair down, looked uncommonly lovely.

He watched her for a long moment, and smiled. "You know, you're very lovely. Just lately, you're...I don't quite know how to put it...you're much more feminine."

Probably because of what Nick had taught her, she thought sadly, and colored a little. She was a woman now, not a nervous spinster. Nick hadn't called, hadn't come over. He was avoiding her, she reckoned, probably afraid because she might read more into last night than he wanted her to. It was just like old times.

"You look lovely," Daniel was saying, his eyes on her.

"Thank you, Daniel."

"Are you sure you don't want to get engaged again?" he murmured as he eased her onto her back and loomed over her. "It would be no hardship at all to marry you. Tabitha, you're lovely...!"

He bent and kissed her, very gently. She smiled and reached up to his shoulders to push him away.

But that wasn't how it looked to the angry man who'd just opened the front door without knocking, incensed to find Daniel's car in Tabby's driveway when he'd come back from visiting his friend at FBI headquarters.

Tabby and Daniel heard the door open at the same time and looked toward it.

Nick was almost vibrating with fury. His dark eyes flashed, his deep tan reddened as he glared at the two on the floor. His big, lean hand clenched on the doorknob until the knuckles went white.

"You vicious tease!" he accused Tabby. "Is that all it meant to you? I suppose the engagement is back on again?"

Daniel didn't understand the accusation, but Tabby did. She sat up, flushing. "Nick..."

"Well, don't mind me," he said coldly. "You know where I stand. I've never made any secret of the fact that forever after isn't my style."

She knew, but she'd hoped. Her eyes narrowed with sadness. "Yes, I know, Nick," she said quietly.

Her reasonable tone made him even more furious. The fact that dear Daniel was rumpled and had lipstick on his mouth sent him right through the roof. "It was fun," he told Tabby. "But a little too tame for my taste. Maybe Dr. Myers here is more your cup of tea. I wish you both all the best."

"What are you implying?" Daniel asked, ruffled, as he got to his feet.

"What do you think?" he asked, glaring at Tabby, who was scrambling to her feet. "I thought you weren't the kind of woman to go from one man to another in two days. What a chump I was!"

"Nick, I didn't!" she cried, astonished at the sudden realization that he was jealous. He thought she was two-timing him. Perhaps the hurtful things he was saying arose out of jealousy in the first place, and he . . . *cared!* "Listen to me . . . !"

"I've heard more than enough," he told her implacably. "Goodbye, Tabby."

He went back out, slamming the door. Tabby, horrified that she might have made the biggest mistake of her life, ran after him. She opened the door and sprinted across the lawn that separated her house from his.

"Nick, wait!" she called in exasperation.

"Leave me alone," he growled over his shoulder.

People mowing lawns stopped and watched the sight of their very correct neighbor, Dr. Harvey, apparently chasing a man, and dressed in a very skimpy outfit, too. The men stared admiringly at her long, tanned legs. She'd never before ventured off her patio in shorts.

"Nick, I love you!" she cried.

"No, you don't. You love that stuffed shirt!" he raged. "You only used me for sex!"

She gasped as she realized that his deep voice was carrying, and that her grinning neighbors were having a field day. She blushed furiously.

"How dare you!" she yelled at him. "How dare you say things like that to me in public!"

He whirled at his front door, his eyes blazing. "Go back to your egghead over there and see if he can make you scream your head off the way I did in bed!"

She covered her face with her hands. "I'll never forgive you!"

Nick looked around at the neighborhood audience, cold mockery in the smile that flared on his handsome face. "Ruined your spotless reputation, have I?" he asked coldly. "Well, that's what you get for seducing innocent men and then dropping them when someone else comes along!"

"I didn't seduce you!"

"Fudge." He opened his door.

"Will you please listen!" she burst out.

"Sure. Like you listened to me last night." He slammed the door in her face.

She hesitated for a minute. Then she went up to the door and knocked and knocked. He ignored her. She called. He still ignored her. She called again and knocked until her knuckles were raw and her voice was hoarse. Finally she kicked it, with no response. Then she went to the window, to try to get his attention. He pulled the curtains together with a furious jerk.

"Damn you, Nick!" she yelled, tears of angry frustration in her eyes. "I wouldn't marry you if you had buckets of money and covered me in precious jewels!"

The door opened. "I don't marry fickle women," he told her coldly. "You two-timing Jezebel!"

"Look who's talking!" she shouted. "The playboy of the western world!"

"At least I was reformed! You're just getting started!" He glared toward a shocked Daniel, who was standing in the grass getting an earful. "Go marry your writing collaborator. I don't want you!"

"You did!" she threw back.

"Only for one night," he said with cold pleasure when she flushed. "It was nice, but I've had better. And I will again. Go home!"

He slammed the door for the second time. Tabby cursed. She never had in her life, but she cursed steadily at the top of her lungs, while all around her, male neighbors chuckled and began to form groups.

Wives came out of their kitchens to see what all the fuss was about. Tabby, who'd always been so correct and proper and self-conscious, didn't give a damn if the whole world heard her. She told Nick what she thought of him, called him every foul name she'd ever heard in English and two foreign languages. Finally, when she was weak from it all, she stormed back to her own house, past Daniel, and into the house.

"Uh, Tabby, it might be a good idea if we didn't work on the book tonight."

She looked at Daniel. "Yes," she said, realizing belatedly that he was actually intimidated by her unfettered temper. Amazing. He seemed so self-possessed, but feminine rage unmanned him. It hadn't fazed Nick. She grimaced. "Sorry about that."

He put on his shoes and his tie and jacket with a rueful smile. "Well, no need asking how you feel about Mr. Reed anymore. I wish you luck, Tabby. It would be a pity to waste that kind of emotion on me."

"I'm sorry," she said again, helplessly.

He kissed her forehead gently. "I'll enjoy working on the book with you," he said. He actually laughed. "And I thought you were cold. My, my."

She flushed. "Good night, Daniel."

"Good night, Tabby. I'll phone you tomorrow."

She nodded, watching him go without any real misgivings. She glared at Nick's house. The neighbors were still glancing her way. No more floor show today, folks, she thought, closing the door. Incredible, she mused, that she felt no shame or regret for her rage outside. Nick had certainly changed her, and not necessarily for the better. Being a scarlet woman was invigorating, if nothing else.

The guilt would go eventually, she supposed. Meanwhile, she punched in Nick's number several times over the course of the evening. He wouldn't pick up the receiver. Finally she slammed it down and went to bed. All right, if that was how he wanted it. He could sulk all night. Tomorrow, she'd try again. If he cared about her that much, that he lost every bit of his self-control in temper, then there was definitely hope for them. Even if he was too stubborn to admit it just yet. She was smiling to herself when she went to bed, and she dreamed of babies and Nick reading bedtime stories to them.

Nine

———

Tabby tried once more the next morning to get Nick on the telephone or to the door, but he was being stubborn again. With a reluctant sigh, she went to school, taught her classes and was later called to the dean's office early to hear his apology for placing her under suspension.

"You always believed that I was innocent," she replied with a warm smile. "Even though I was the most likely suspect. You only did what you had to do to protect the school."

"There were other suspects, you know," he said surprisingly. "I have to admit that two of the faculty were high on my list, but I'm glad to find that our thief was small and hairy!"

"So am I!" Tabby agreed. "I hope I still have a job...?"

"Don't be absurd," he said, smiling at her. He rose and shook her hand. "You're one of the best educators we've ever employed. I would have been devastated to lose you."

It was a politically correct thing to say, but she knew that he meant it. She smiled back glowingly. "I would have been very sad to leave here. I learned just how much my work meant to me during all this."

"It usually takes a crisis to make us appreciate the value of things we sometimes take for granted," he agreed.

Yes, she thought, remembering Nick's odd behavior. Why hadn't she realized that his loss of control with her, both times, could have had its roots in deep emotion? Her naïveté had kept her from seeing his involvement until it was almost too late. But there was still hope, if she could reach him and make him talk to her. She could have kicked herself for walking away that night he'd wanted to talk.

She'd planned to corner him that night. But when she got home, the house next door was closed up and the rental car was gone. Minutes after she'd fixed herself a sandwich and a cup of coffee, a power company truck arrived to cut off the electricity. She knew then that Nick had gone. Without another word, without a real goodbye, even without a note, he'd faded away and she was alone again. She'd left it too late. He'd closed the door and no matter if she tried to phone him or write to him in Houston, she knew it would do no good. It was over. He'd told her so without out a single word.

She was too depressed to do much after that. She ate her meager fare and sat around trying to grade test papers, but eventually she went to bed and cried herself to sleep. Nick had decided that he didn't want her. He'd seduced her and had his fill, and she'd given in and let him. Now he was on his way back to Houston, to his job and his friends. Tabby had been relegated to the faceless crowd of his ex-lovers, just like all the rest.

She stopped thinking about it because she couldn't bear it. But as the days went by, her face began to show the ravages of her nights. She grew wan and pale, and listless. Her enthusiasm for her job dimmed. She went through the motions of living without really caring whether she did or not.

A week later, one worry was dispensed with. She had proof that she wasn't pregnant, and she almost jumped for joy. She wanted children, but not out of wedlock. Love on one side was never enough. She'd thought Nick might really care deeply about her, but if he did, he'd have been in touch by now. He simply wasn't interested. She had to face that.

She debated about calling Nick and telling him there was nothing to worry about, but she decided against it when she didn't hear anything from him. He was obviously not concerned with what had become of her, so let him continue in his oblivion.

Actually, Nick was oblivious only because he was being worked to death. Lassiter, sensing his employee's violent emotional state upon his return, had immediately thrown him in headfirst on a kidnapping case. For the past week he'd been on the road, trying to track down a parent who'd absconded with his four-year-old son while his ex-wife tried frantically to find him.

Nick had finally turned him up in a flea-bitten motel outside a small New Mexico town. He'd persuaded the desperate father to turn himself in, for the child's sake. That hadn't been an easy task, but he'd accomplished it.

All the time, he'd thought about Tabby and wished that he hadn't been so bullheaded when she'd tried to explain why she and Daniel had been making love on her carpet. Now he was worried about her. She was deeply religious and he'd seduced her. She might even be pregnant. What if she did something desperate because he wouldn't listen? When he got back to Houston, the first thing he did was ask his sister if she'd heard from her best friend.

"No," she said quizzically. "Should I have?"

"I thought she might have phoned to tell you how things were going, now that she's been cleared," he replied tersely.

Helen pursed her lips. She knew her brother. He looked haggard and guilty, and she'd already guessed that something devastating had happened to him in D.C. It had to involve Tabby, but she couldn't guess what it was.

"Why don't you call her, if you're so curious?" she asked.

He turned away. "I've got another case to start on," he replied. "I haven't time."

"I've got cases of my own," she reminded him, "but it doesn't take five minutes to pick up a telephone and make a call, does it?"

"Never mind," he said irritably.

She watched him storm out of the office with new interest. He was worried about Tabby for some reason, but he wasn't willing to phone her. Why? Wouldn't she talk to him, was that it?

That night Helen telephoned Tabby. Nick was out of town again on a new case, and there was probably no doubt that he hadn't been burning up telephone lines.

"How are you?" Helen asked without preamble. "Nick wouldn't say why, but he seemed to be worried about you."

Tabby felt her heart leap involuntarily. "I'm fine," she said noncommittally. "If he asks, you can tell him there isn't anything he needs to be concerned about. He needn't waste any of his valuable time being worried about me!"

That sounded vicious. Helen grinned. "How's Daniel?"

"He and I are still working on our book. Unfortunately he's discovered that I have a temper. He doesn't want to marry me anymore. Just as well," she said, "because I think I hate men now!"

"You broke the engagement?"

"Yes. Daniel is a fine man, but he deserves more than I have to give him."

"You sound different," Helen said with some concern.

"I suppose I am different," Tabby told her. "I've had a hard couple of weeks, through no fault of my own. I've learned some lessons that hurt."

That sounded vaguely ominous. "Anything to do with Nick?"

"I'm finally convinced that he'll never be desperately in love with me, if that's what you mean." Tabby laughed bitterly. "He gave me the cure. I tried to talk to him and he left D.C. without a word or a note or even a goodbye."

"I'm sorry," Helen said sincerely. "He's been different since he's been back. I'd hoped it might be because of you."

"Not a chance. He can't see me for dust. It's probably just as well. Now that I think about it, I'm sure I wouldn't be happy with a man who can't live without a different woman in his bed every night and a gun under his pillow!"

"He doesn't date anybody these days," Helen remarked. "Not since New Year's, in fact. Isn't that odd?"

Tabby refused to let herself hope. She'd had enough misery on Nick's account.

"He hasn't even been talking anymore about being restless and changing jobs," Helen added.

"That's probably why he's thinking of going with the DEA or the customs people," Tabby muttered. "He said he was."

"Funny, he didn't mention it around here."

"He'll get around to it. I have to go. I've got a lot of papers to grade."

"Sure. Well, keep in touch, will you? I worry about you."

Tabby smiled. "I know. I worry about you, too, believe it or not. You're the only family I have left, even if you aren't a blood relation."

"That goes double for me. I'm sorry my brother is such a blind idiot."

"He's that, all right! Blind, deaf, dumb and stupid as a . . . !" She forced herself to calm down when she heard Helen's faint giggle. "It wouldn't have worked, anyway. I hardly fit the image of the glamorous party girl with a laid-back attitude toward love."

"Yes, I see what you mean," Helen said ruefully.

"Just tell your stupid brother that he doesn't have anything to worry about. *If* he bothers to ask," she added venomously.

"I'll do that little thing. You take care of yourself."

"You, too."

Helen hung up, her mind going like a watch. Tabby sounded different. Something was going on. She had to make Nick tell her what it was, since Tabby wouldn't.

But she didn't get a chance the next day. Nick didn't come back. However, a complication did upset the routine of the office.

Harold proposed immediate marriage. Helen, astonished, agreed on the spot, only to be told that Harold was going to have to move to South America for a year to work on his father's construction gang as a prerequisite to inheriting his trust fund.

"What am I going to do?" Helen wailed to Tess Lassiter later that day. "I hate to put you on the spot like this, but I love Harold. I want to go with him. We have to get married now and leave the country in a week."

"You're irreplaceable," Tess agreed. "But I can see that you have to go with Harold. Don't worry," she said gently. "Something will work out."

Something did, hours later. A weeping Kit Morris, Tess's best friend, came storming into the office with red eyes and audible sobs.

"He fired me!" she choked, going into Tess's outstretched arms.

"He? You mean Logan Deverell, your boss?" Tess asked, aghast. "But you've worked for him for three years . . . !"

"Slaved for him," Kit amended, wiping her big blue eyes. Her oval face in its frame of dark hair was as white as tissue except for her red nose. "But he's got a new lady love. She was terrible to me. We had an argument. She threw hot coffee all over me, and he took her side and he told me to get out and that he didn't want to have to see me ever again!"

Tess was astonished. Kit had worked for Logan Deverell for longer than Tess had worked with Dane before she married him. The two were inseparable during working hours and sometimes even at evening soirees where Kit was obliged to take notes for her boss. Now Logan had apparently fired her over some woman. It was almost too much to believe.

"What am I going to do?" Kit wailed. "I've got rent due, and a car payment, and he didn't say one word about severance pay. I've got no place to go, and not even a job...!" She started crying again.

Tess thought about her problem, and about the agency's problem of losing Helen so quickly. She smiled as she began to arrive at a solution to both their problems.

"Kit," she asked her best friend, "have you ever thought about doing detective work?"

Nick was finally on his way back home again. He'd pursued a bail jumper all the way to San Francisco, only to lose him to a streetcar. The man had underestimated its speed and fallen under its metal mass, dying instantly. Nick had watched. The man had been young, much younger than himself. The experience had shaken and sobered him—much the same as when he'd lost Lucy—making him realize just how short life was. He saw the world through new, more cynical eyes, and he began to see things that he hadn't before. He was going to die someday himself. If he did, would anyone really care except his sister? He was practically alone. No wife, no family, no one of his own to love. No one—except Tabby. She'd wanted to love him so badly, but he wouldn't let her. Now he'd faced mortality; he'd seen death. Everything had changed, all at once.

There was, he decided, no point in continuing to hide his head in the sand. Tabby was a part of his life that he wasn't going to be happy without. He didn't want roots, but it looked as if he had them just the same. He hadn't looked at another woman since he'd had Tabby. He didn't want anyone else.

The thing was, he'd behaved like an idiot. How did Tabby feel after the way he'd treated her? He groaned out loud at the memory of the things he'd said to her, and how she'd reacted to them. Chances were very good that she'd go off the deep end and marry prissy Daniel just to show him. He'd fouled up everything with his callous attitude.

He got off the plane in Houston and took a cab to the office. He reported to Dane and heard Helen's news without really comprehending it.

"Didn't you understand?" his sister asked irritably. "I'm marrying Harold and going off to South America, to the jungle, where pygmies live!"

"That's Africa," he murmured absently.

"Headhunters, then!"

"Wear a scarf and keep it tied," he advised.

She threw up her hands. "What's the matter with you!"

He looked at her, his hands deep in his pockets, glad that they were temporarily undisturbed in his office. "Did you talk to Tabby?"

She shifted her stance. "Yes. Why?" she added, cocking her head.

"How is she?" he asked.

"She sounded strange," she began.

His face began to pale. He caught her by the shoulders. "Suicidally depressed?" he persisted.

"No!" She frowned at him. "In fact, she sounded more mature and independent than ever."

His lips parted on a held breath. "Helen, is she pregnant?" he asked in a choked tone, his eyes wild as they searched hers.

Light bulbs went on in her head. So that was it! Her eyes widened and she smiled. "Well, well," she mused.

He actually flushed. He dropped his hands and moved away, staring out the window with the first embarrassment he could ever remember feeling. "She'd have told you, surely, if she was?"

"She's not," she said, sorry to put him out of his misery so quickly. She'd enjoyed seeing her big, strong brother just momentarily weak.

"You witch!" he burst out, turning, his dark eyes blazing at her. "You might have spared me!"

"Why?" she asked reasonably. "Tabby wouldn't tell me anything. I wanted to know why she was so sarcastic about you. Almost as if she hated you. She told me to tell you that you had absolutely nothing to be concerned about. I wondered what it meant." She grinned. "Now I know."

The flush got worse. "Don't push."

"Sorry. Going to marry her?" she persisted, and her eyes narrowed. "You don't go around seducing nice girls like Tabby," she added. "It's ungentlemanly."

"I know that, too," he replied heavily. "Believe me, it wasn't anything I planned. I loused it all up," he added, throwing up his hands. "Just like I did before, at New Year's. She'll never believe another thing I say. She'll never trust me."

"You could go back and try to talk to her," Helen suggested.

He glared at her furiously. "You conned me into going home before. That's what got me into this mess."

"Tabby loves you. Love doesn't die because of a few harsh words."

"I wouldn't be too sure of that. It might have been nothing more than a long-standing infatuation."

"And it might not. You could—"

"Where the *hell* have you put my secretary?" came a deep roar from the direction of the open office door.

Nick and Helen turned together to find a huge, dark-haired, dark-eyed man glowering at them. He was dressed in a green overcoat and his thick hair was wet. His deeply tanned face was livid with anger. One huge hand was holding the door open, and the other was holding a cigar.

"If you mean Kit," Helen said, "she's out with Tess and Dane."

"Doing what?" he demanded.

"Eating lunch, I guess." Helen shrugged. "Did you need to see her about something?"

"Something." He nodded. "She hid my appointment book before she left and messed up the computer. Every time I hit a button, it throws up an error message at me! I'm going to wring her neck!''

Helen exchanged glances with Nick. ''Tell you what, Mr. Deverell,'' she offered, ''I'll come back with you and fix the computer. I think I know what's wrong with it. As for Kit, she'll be back about two, I suppose.''

''Back here? Why?'' he demanded.

''They gave her a job,'' Helen said and winced when he proceeded to turn the air blue.

Long minutes later, Helen managed to persuade Logan Deverell back into his own office. It wouldn't do for poor Kit to have to confront him in this violent temper.

What was wrong with the computer, she soon discovered, was Logan Deverell. He didn't know how to use it. Within minutes, she extracted all the information he needed and managed to get an agency to send over a sacrificial victim to do his office work. Then she got out, quickly.

Nick had gone back to his apartment in the meantime, smoking one cigarette after another until he had a vicious cough.

He threw the package on the floor and stepped on it finally and then jerked up the telephone and dialed Washington, D.C.

Tabby had only been home from work for about fifteen minutes. She was still recuperating from her long day with a cup of coffee when the phone rang.

Daniel, probably, she thought wryly as she picked it up, wanting her to do some more research for his book. She wouldn't mind. It gave her a way to fill in the emptiness of her life without Nick.

"Hello?" she asked with twinkling amusement.

The sound of her voice made Nick's heart catch. He felt as if he'd come home. He leaned back in his easy chair and kicked his shoes off. "Hello, Tabby," he said quietly.

She almost put the receiver down.

"Don't hang up," he asked softly. "I haven't called to hassle you. I just want to know."

"About what?" she said curtly, making it hard for him.

"If you're carrying my child," he replied gently.

There was a long pause. "No, I'm not," she said stiffly. "I told Helen to tell you..."

"Yes. She did."

"Then why are you calling me?"

"To make sure there were no misunderstandings," he said simply. "How are you?"

"I'm very well, thanks," she bit off.

"Want to know how I am?" he asked with bitter sarcasm.

"Only if you've had your head blown off or you've got termites in your wooden heart," she said icily.

"Funny girl."

"I've told you how I am."

"So you have. How about flying out here?"

"What for?" she asked coldly.

He stared around at the apartment, and saw for the first time how empty and dull it was. There was no color, no life, in it. "I thought you might like to spruce up my apartment. Make it livable."

"I'd dig a hole and fill it with crocodiles..."

"Venomous," he sighed. "I don't suppose I blame you. I've been a twenty-four karat heel. For what it's worth, I was feeling betrayed, although God knows why I should when I gave you every reason to want to put a knife in my pride. I ran, but you were everywhere I went."

"You don't have to feel threatened because of me," she told him, aching inside. Why did he have to call now and destroy her hard-won peace of mind?

"I close my eyes and see you, Tabby," he said softly. "Feel you. Taste you."

"Me and the rest of the women in the country..."

"I haven't had anyone since I had you," he said quietly. "I won't. Not ever again."

She hesitated. It was a line. Just a line. She had to force herself to accept that. She closed her eyes. "It won't work. I don't want you, Nick. I'm..." She searched for a lie. "I'm going to marry Daniel."

"That wasn't what you told Helen," he said smugly.

She let out a rough sigh. "I'll never tell her anything else as long as I live, you can bet on that!"

"Buy a plane ticket. Come out here," he coaxed. His voice dropped. "Live with me, Tabby."

She had to clench her teeth to bite back an answer. It was tempting. Oh, yes, it was tempting. But living with a man didn't figure in her scheme of things. She wanted a wedding ring and a settled marriage. She wanted children. Nick was only offering an affair.

"No," she whispered hoarsely. "I can't do that, Nick."

"Why?" he asked, his voice more tender than she'd ever heard it.

"It wouldn't work. I'm not... not suited to fervent affairs. I can't come, Nick."

"Affairs...?"

"There's someone at the door," she lied unsteadily. "I have to go." She hung up and then took the phone off the hook.

Tears rolled down her cheeks in torrents. She threw herself down on the couch and bawled. Why had he called, to torment her with temptations she had to resist? As much as she loved him, she could have strangled him for that!

Nick was staring at the receiver with a scowl. What had brought on that comment about having an affair with him, he wondered. He'd asked her to come and live with him....

He slapped his forehead roughly. Of all the stupid things, he'd let her think he wanted her to come and live with him without offering her marriage. Having seduced her twice without mentioning any kind of commitment, how could he blame her for not trusting him? His Tabby would never consent to such living arrangements. She was too conventional for unconventional relationships.

Well, it would be easy enough to clarify that. He dialed the number again. Busy. He kept trying, but she'd obviously taken it off the hook. Just the way he'd done to her before he left D.C. Oddly enough, he didn't get angry. She was entitled to a little revenge.

He gave up at midnight and called the airlines. There was only one way to handle it now. He was going to have to go up and see her. In person, he had a much better chance of making her change her mind.

He caught a plane out early the next morning. Kit and Helen watched him leave the office after speaking to Dane.

"Good luck!" Helen called after him.

"Thanks," he murmured dryly. "I'll need it!"

"So will you," Helen murmured to Kit as a taller, bigger male form replaced Nick's in the doorway and marched in.

Kit paled, but she lifted her chin stubbornly. "I'm not coming back," she told Logan Deverell. "As far as I'm concerned, you can make your own coffee and type your own letters for the rest of your life!"

"You don't think you can be replaced?" he mused coldly. "At this very moment, I have a very capable new secretary sorting out the *mess* you made of my filing system!"

She stiffened. "Your filing system came out of a book! It's the very latest thing..."

"No damned kidding?" he asked sarcastically. "Amazing that I can't find a single file using it!"

"People who can spell," she said pointedly, "find it very simple."

His dark eyes glittered. He jammed his hands into his slacks pockets, stretching them across the powerful muscles of his thighs. His broad face showed no emotion at all as he looked at her.

"I came by," he said, "to tell you that you left your vegetation in my office in your haste to depart. I'd appreciate having it removed."

"Gladly," she told him. "I'd hate for it to die of poison from those corn shucks you smoke."

"Imported cigars," he corrected.

"They always smelled like corn shucks to me," she said cheerfully. "The masks are in my top drawer, if your new secretary can't take the fumes."

He stared at her without blinking, his very posture intimidating. Kit was tall, but he was taller. Her blue eyes met his dark ones without flinching, but they fell before the arrogant contempt in his.

"You owe me two weeks' notice," he told her.

"Which you'd have gotten if you hadn't thrown a book at me!"

"I didn't throw it. It fell."

"Six feet, horizontally?"

He drew in a rough breath. "What are you going to do in here?" he asked suddenly, glancing around. "Type letters or answer the phone?"

"Neither," she informed him smugly. "I'm going to be a detective."

The laughter that burst from his lips made her flush wildly. "You stop that!" she raged. "It isn't funny!"

He lit a cigar and shook his head as he started back out the door. "Miss Private Eye. Now I've heard everything. You can't even find your car keys when you get ready to leave the office. How are you going to find a missing person?"

"I'll be good at it! At least I won't have to put up with you anymore, Mount Vesuvius!"

His powerful shoulders shrugged. "Poor Dane." He went out and closed the door.

"I had to go and help him work the computer after you left yesterday," Helen confided amusedly. "He couldn't spell the commands. The computer shut down on him."

"Good!"

"Why did he fire you?" Helen asked, frowning. "My goodness, you've worked for him forever."

"I told him his newest conquest had taken her former lover for everything he had. He was a neighbor of mine. He...almost killed himself," she said, grimacing. "I was trying to warn Mr. Deverell. Some fat chance. He makes up his mind, and it's like an edict from Mount Olympus!" she yelled at the closed door.

"HE IMMEDIATELY GOES DEAF WHEN HE MAKES UP HIS MIND!"

"Experience is the best teacher," Helen reminded her gently.

"What a nice saying. I'll have it engraved and give it to him for Christmas. It may be the only thing of value he'll have left by then," she added with a cold smile.

Helen didn't say another word. But she had a feeling that this feud was far from over. Meanwhile, she hoped her brother was going to be lucky enough to get Tabby back. It would be a real pity if he finally admitted his feelings and it was too late. Nick had always been a free agent, but he'd been noticeably different since he'd come back from D.C. And if anyone could make him settle down, it was Tabby.

Ten

Nick rented a car at the airport in D.C. and drove quickly back to his father's old house. It was Saturday now and Tabby would be home. He was counting on the chance that she'd be home alone, and that Daniel wouldn't be anywhere around. He needed to talk to her in private, without any prying eyes. He hoped that would be possible, remembering what an interesting spectacle they'd presented to her amused neighbors the last time he was here.

It wasn't going to be easy. He knew that already. He'd put his freedom and independence above Tabby's pride. He'd treated her shamefully and if she couldn't forgive him, he really didn't know what he was going to do.

He parked the car in the driveway and sat in it for a long moment, gathering up the courage to face her.

Finally he got out and started for her front door. But on an impulse, he turned and went around the house.

She was lying on a chaise longue on her small patio, wearing a one-piece bathing suit that highlighted her lovely figure. He stared at her hungrily, remembering how it had felt to make love to her. His body went taut all at once and he smiled ruefully at his own impatience.

Perhaps, he thought, the element of surprise would give him an edge. He was going to need one.

He moved around the chair and suddenly straddled it just as Tabby's eyes opened and dilated.

"Guess who?" he mused, and lowered his body completely onto hers.

She gasped. "Nick . . . !"

He smiled as she tried to push him off. He wouldn't let her. His long legs entangled with hers, slowly caressing their bare length as his mouth went down over hers. He began to kiss her slowly, warmly, with aching tenderness. He didn't touch her at all.

"It's broad daylight," she squeaked when he paused to get a breath of air, overwhelmed by his ardor and her helpless need of him. It had been so long. She'd missed him beyond bearing. Her eyes stared up into his with aching adoration.

He didn't miss the warmth in her look. "So it is. Have I ever told you how utterly lovely you are?" he asked softly. He smiled and bent to her mouth again. "Remind me to do that when I stop aching. Put your hands on my hips and hold me against you, Tabby. I hurt like hell."

"The neighbors . . ." she protested under his mouth.

"They're all watching television," he whispered, levering down between her legs. "Yes," he said unsteadily. "Yes, that feels good, doesn't it?" He pushed, and she gasped and blushed.

The intimacy was shattering. He lifted his head and looked into her eyes, searching them tenderly while he shifted lazily from one side to the other and watched her try to breathe.

"Nick, stop," she protested, and then gave up, her eyes hungry on his face even as she fought to keep her pride intact. "Oh, why did you have to come back!" she raged miserably. "I was just beginning to get over you!"

"No, you weren't," he said knowingly. "No more than I was beginning to get over you. We're stuck with each other, baby. I think I knew that for certain at that New Year's Eve party. That's why I've been the devil to get along with ever since."

"You only want me to live with you...!"

He kissed her mouth shut, very gently. "Yes. For the rest of my life. The rest of yours. I want to marry you, Tabby," he breathed into her parted lips as he slowly increased the pressure of his kiss.

She went under. All her dreams were coming true. She clung to him, oblivious to the whole world. "You went away. You wouldn't answer your phone," she whispered.

"Neither would you, last night. I had to come all this way just to make you listen. Are you listening?" he teased gently. "I want you for keeps. I was afraid of that kind of bond between us, but I'm not afraid anymore," he added grimly. "Seeing you on the floor with darling Daniel convinced me of that in ten seconds flat!"

"It wasn't what you thought," she told him. "Really it wasn't. He was kissing me, not vice versa."

"Who could blame him, really," Nick sighed, looking at her lovely body with possessive eyes. "I know how it feels to hold you like that. The difference was," he added firmly, "that you belong to me. I was your first man, your only man. I mean to be your last man, too."

"You reformed rakes," she managed, laughing.

"We make good husbands and fathers," he informed her. "Marry me, and I'll show you." He pursed his lips and studied her flat belly with intense interest. "I don't know that I mind the thought of deliberately making a baby with you. In fact," he added, touching her stomach with one big, lean hand as he held her eyes, "it excites me. Want to see?"

She cleared her throat and sat up as the man next door began to start his lawnmower. The thing was, he wasn't looking at his lawnmower, he was looking at Tabby. "Better not," she said, glancing past him.

He lifted his head and gave the man a hard glare. Immediately the neighbor began to mow through his wife's flower bed.

"Shame on you!" she exclaimed.

"I don't like him staring at you," he said possessively.

"You jealous man, you."

"I can't help it. You're mine. I tried to keep my distance, after New Year's Eve. You really got to me, and I was afraid of going in headfirst. But when I came back here, I just lost it altogether. What happened in the park that day was inevitable." He winced at her expression. "That, I regret most of all. But I don't regret what came after it," he added fervently. "That night we had together was the most beautiful night of my life."

She felt those words all the way into her heart. "You left," she reminded him.

"I had to. I was so jealous of Daniel that all I could think about was how his head would look in a bowl. I knew by then that it was more than physical with me. But I thought you'd decided that I wasn't worth the risk of your heart. Maybe I was afraid to try to convince you," he added honestly. "I had mixed feelings about being faithful for the rest of my life. Not anymore," he added quietly. "I have no doubts left."

"You know I'm not pregnant," she blurted out. "I told Helen..."

"Yes." He smiled faintly. "I'll have hell living that down, believe me. But just for the record, I do want children. I'm glad that there won't be a baby just yet, though," he said seriously. "Children shouldn't be accidents."

"No," she agreed softly, smiling at him. "They should be wanted, by both people."

He touched her hair gently. "And not born out of wedlock, either."

"No."

"So, that being the case," he breathed against her mouth, "I think I'd better marry you before we try to make one."

He held her gently and kissed her until she was breathless. "I care deeply for you," he said huskily. "You know that, don't you?"

Caring wasn't loving, but it was a start. He wanted her enough to give up his freedom for her. It would be a chance, but she'd already faced life without him. It was less than pleasant.

"You might regret marrying me one day," she began worriedly.

"That works both ways. Marriage is what you make of it."

"I suppose so."

"How will you feel about giving up your job here to live in Houston?"

She started. "I hadn't considered that." It disturbed her. She had put in a lot of time and one day she might head her department. It would mean giving up a lot.

He chuckled softly. "Never mind. I can see that the idea doesn't appeal. To tell you the truth, I'm a little tired of Houston. I'd like to come home to D.C. There's always enough business for a private detective in this neck of the woods. And it's handy to FBI headquarters."

She looked horrified.

He smoothed out her frown. "I'm not going back there," he assured her. "Or to DEA or the customs service, if you're brooding about that. I like detective work enough. I don't want you worrying all the time."

Her heart lifted. "I would never have asked you to give it up," she said.

"I know that. But it would have kept you upset."

"I love you," she said huskily, averting her eyes.

His body tingled all over. He looked at her in wonder. "Still?" he asked. "Even after the way I've hurt you?"

"Love doesn't wear out, Nick. It survives almost everything you do to it."

"It must. I've been a real pain, haven't I?"

She smoothed her hands over his broad chest with the first stirrings of possession. "So have I, I guess." She looked up. "Marriage isn't something I can take lightly, though, Nick. I can't marry you on speculation. You know, one of those 'we'll get a divorce if it doesn't work out things.'"

He drew her gently into his arms and held her. "I don't want a fly-by-night marriage, either. I'll settle, baby. You'll have to take me on trust, but I won't sell you out or have women on the side. Does that reassure you?"

"I'm not blond and sophisticated," she reminded him. "I may not fit in very well. We college professor types are pretty much loners by trade, and we feel uncomfortable without our trappings."

"You keep forgetting that I studied law, don't you?" he teased, brushing his mouth over her forehead. "Lawyers are very often staid types, too. In fact, I have to confess that I've spent a lot of the past few years being called a bore. Most women who go out with me expect a dashing hero like the ones they see on television. I'm afraid I don't quite fit the image. I'm not flamboyant and I like to talk about famous criminal cases."

"I love to read old Earl Stanley Gardner novels," she confessed. "He was a lawyer himself."

"I knew that. I'm a Perry Mason addict, too." He drew back, searching her eyes warmly. "See? Something else we have in common. I like kids, too."

She smiled wistfully. "It will work, won't it?" she asked nervously. "I mean, you don't feel as if you're being forced into something you don't want to do?"

"I want to spend every night for the rest of my life in your arms," he replied frankly. "Holding you. Loving you. Showing you how much you matter to me. Does that sound like force to you?"

"Not if you really mean it."

"I mean it, all right," he said fervently, his eyes burning into hers. "God knows, I've never meant anything more."

"It isn't just that you want me?" she persisted.

He eased her away from him and helped her into her robe before he led her back into the house. He held her hand warmly in his big one, his eyes on the door, not on Tabby.

He opened the door and let her inside. "Make some coffee, could you? I came straight here from the airport."

"Certainly." She went into the kitchen and started a pot of coffee brewing. She was all thumbs. It showed. "I never got a bill," she said shakily. "I asked you to send me one."

"A bill?" He shook his head. "Tabby! Are you crazy?"

She smiled at him. "I must be. You seem to be an addiction I can't quite cure."

He put his hands into his pockets to avoid temptation. Then he leaned back against the counter to watch her get down cups and saucers from the cabinet. "You look right at home in the kitchen. Take your hair down."

The request was so sudden that she turned and stared at him.

"I love your hair down your back," he mused. "I used to think you tortured it into that bun because you knew I preferred it loose."

She smiled shyly. "I suppose I might have."

She took it down and shook her head to let it fall in natural waves around her shoulders.

He nodded. "That's better." He glared at her. "You had it down that night you were kissing Daniel."

"Not on purpose," she said, soothing him.

He sighed. "Okay. I've missed you. I thought I hated domesticity." He shrugged with a rueful smile. "I hated being alone more."

"So did I." She fiddled with a spoon.

He arched away from the counter and caught her by the waist, pulling her lazily to him. "It's going to be difficult for me at first," he said seriously. "For you, too, I imagine. Learning to live with another person, at our ages, when we're set in our ways is never easy. But I'll try if you will."

"Nick, I'm not sure..."

He tilted her chin up to his dark eyes. "You love me. That makes you sure." He bent and brushed his mouth lightly over hers. "And just for the record, there won't be any heated lovemaking before we say our vows. I started off badly with you. This time, we'll do the thing right."

Her heart lifted. He looked as if he really meant it. "You sound so conventional," she laughed.

"All that upbringing raising its ugly head," he chided.

"Rules hold civilizations together," she reminded him. "When religion breaks down, so does society. I can quote you examples, not the least of which is the reign of Amenhotep IV who became Akenaton, giving his people one god in a desperate attempt to bring religion back to them. It didn't work. Egypt fell into moral decay not too long after he died and eventually fell prey to other cultures. So," she added, "did most great civilizations. It isn't *if* they end. It's when."

"You pessimist!" he accused.

"When you see how many civilizations have risen and fallen over the centuries, cynicism is inevitable."

She searched his eyes. "But I'm glad that ours is still around. And that you're part of it. And that you want to marry me."

He smiled. "Kiss me. Then feed me some coffee and let's make a few plans."

They did. He had to go back to Houston several days later to fill in while Adams was down with a cold, and Tabby ached at letting him leave. But the wedding was planned for only three days after that. She was to fly out to Houston, so that Helen could be her maid of honor, and they were going to be married in a Presbyterian church that Nick attended infrequently.

"I'll die of loneliness," Tabby moaned when she put him on the plane. It had been a magical time, one of discovery and delight, as they learned about each other all over again. There had been, as he'd promised, no physical interludes. But it had been difficult, because she wanted him as badly as he wanted her. Only by limiting themselves to brief kisses and no time alone had they been able to keep that resolution.

"You'll be on your way to Houston before you know it. But I've got cases to solve, and a pupil to teach. If Kit's going to take over when Helen and I leave, she'll need all the help she can get."

"Is she pretty?" Tabby asked suspiciously, her dark eyes brooding.

"I never noticed," he said honestly. "She's been crazy about Logan Deverell for years. Now she's breaking the ties, and having a bad time of it. Watching Kit gave me some idea of how it must have been for you, breaking your heart over me," he said solemnly. "You won't ever need to do that again."

"Won't I?" she asked quietly. "You aren't marrying me out of pity, are you, Nick?"

He glanced toward the loading ramp. The first-class passengers were almost through boarding. His group was next. "I have to go. No, I don't pity you." He took a deep breath and went for broke, his eyes staring straight into hers. "I love you, damn it," he said through his teeth. "All right? You finally made me say it. Satisfied?"

Her face began to glow. She could have danced on top of the airplane. "Nick," she whispered, and went into his arms. The kiss she gave him almost made his knees buckle.

"Stop that," he choked, pushing her away. He actually flushed and kept his back to the other passengers while he fought for control.

"Well, well." She beamed knowingly.

He glared at her. "Just don't gloat," he muttered. "I hate women who gloat."

"I can't help it. I feel dangerous." She made a growling sound in her throat. "Let's make love on the floor."

He actually moaned. "I'm going back to Houston. I'm leaving right now!" He picked up his bag, carrying it strategically. "I'll expect you day after tomorrow."

"Oh, I'll be there," she said, peeking up at him demurely. "I bought this black lace nightgown. It's see-through..."

He kissed her quickly and ran for it.

"Coward!" she called after him.

He grinned over his shoulder as he sprinted down the loading ramp. Then he was out of sight and Tabby was hugging his revelation to her like a teddy bear. Her feet barely touched the ground all the way back to the car.

Eleven

What seemed like a hundred years later—but actually only three days after Nick flew back to Houston—Nick and Tabby became man and wife in a small, intimate ceremony at the local Presbyterian church in Houston.

Tess and Dane, Helen and Harold, and the rest of the staff were there for the occasion. Kit Morris came with Tess. She still looked drawn and pale, but Nick was very pleased with the way she'd taken to detective work. Her boss's loss was the agency's gain, because she had a sweet personality and a way of talking to people that made them anxious to give her any information she asked for. She had a natural compassion, as well, and a steely inner toughness. He felt sorry for Logan Deverell. The man had set loose a treasure.

After the reception, Kit came up to congratulate her mentor. "I hope you're both going to be so happy," she told Tabby, her blue eyes soft and warm. "Nick's a nice man."

"Thank you," Tabby said, smiling. She looked lovely in her oyster-white wedding dress with its Juliet sleeves and V neckline trimmed with lace. She'd worn a long white veil of illusion lace that Nick had lifted with trembling hands just before he kissed her. It was pushed back over the dainty seed-pearled crown of flowers that held it in place.

She looked lovely. Nick had said so twenty times. Now he said it again.

"Let's go," he said softly. "I'm starving to death."

"There's some cake left," she murmured dryly.

His eyes darkened as they searched hers. "It will take something much sweeter than cake to satisfy this particular hunger. Think you can?"

Her lips parted on a breath of pure excitement. "I don't know," she whispered. "But I'm going to love trying."

His face flushed a little. "Let's go, darling. I want you to myself now."

She clasped his big hand in hers and they said their goodbyes. They were flying down to the Cayman Islands for a honeymoon, but tonight they booked a suite in a local luxury hotel. Nick drove them there and swept her up to their rooms without extricating the luggage.

"My things," she protested when he closed the door.

"Later," he breathed as he drew her to him. His eyes burned into her face. "Much, much later. Right now, you won't need clothes, I promise you."

He eased her out of the beautiful wedding gown, whispering how lovely she looked, how much he loved her, needed her. She let him guide her shy hands to his body and teach her new ways to touch him, to make him even hungrier than he already was.

Minutes later, they twisted feverishly against each other on the coverlet of the bed, both nude, both in anguish from their sobbing need.

She was crying when he moved slowly above her and held her eyes while his hips very tenderly eased down. He possessed her completely in one smooth, delicate motion, and she gasped at the feel of it.

"It isn't...like it was...before," she managed, trembling.

"I love you," he said unsteadily. "Love you to the height of the world, the depth of the oceans. I didn't know how much until these last terrible weeks without you. This," he breathed, moving gently so that she gasped at the power of his need, "is how much I need you—!"

His voice broke. His mouth covered hers and he groaned as her hands slid hungrily down his back to the base of his spine. He moved, and she moved with him, in a rhythm that was terrible in its slow, sweet intensity. She sobbed, clung, as they drifted into realms they'd never touched before. It was so slow that she began to cry out as she tried to get closer to him and knew that she could never get as close as she wanted, needed, to get...!

She cried out, her voice throbbing in time with his as the deep, tearing spasms caught them both. He stilled, but his body didn't, couldn't. He shuddered and his voice broke on her name as he gave in to the red waves that scalded him.

Tabby cried for a long time afterward. She wouldn't let him go, cradling him to her, savoring the heat and dampness and even the weight of his powerful body in the aftermath.

"I thought I might die," she whispered unsteadily, staring over his shoulder at the ceiling.

"Now you know why the French call it the little death," he said quietly. He lifted his head, searching her wide eyes. He kissed her eyelids, rubbing the tip of his tongue against the spiky wetness of her thick dark lashes. "This is profound," he whispered. "I never realized that it could be like this with someone."

She opened her eyes. "You were experienced," she began, surprised.

"I never loved anyone until now," he said simply. "With you, it's...more spiritual than physical. I loved you. You loved me. It was a physical expression of something intangible." He touched her face in wonder. "I remember thinking I was going to die trying to get closer to you. Even...that close...wasn't enough."

"Yes," she said, her face mirroring her own awe. "I know."

He drew in a breath and laughed unsteadily. "And this is only the beginning," he said, shivering.

He was afraid! She read that in his face. She touched him gently. "It's all right," she said softly. "I'll never leave you. I'll love you until I die."

He stiffened and his face went taut. And then she knew.

She reached up and kissed him, kissed his eyelids, his cheeks, his nose, his chin. She kissed his mouth with soft reassurance. "I'm not going to do anything foolhardy and get myself shot, you know," she whispered.

He made a sound that barely registered, and his arms became bruising, painful as he held her with something bordering on desperation. "If I lose you, I'll die," he choked.

"Oh, my darling, you're not going to lose me!" she cried, her body trembling as she realized just how deeply he did care for her. "Never, never...Nick, love me...!"

She kissed him, moving her hips under him, arousing him to a sudden, violent frenzy. He lost control and took her with such raging need that she found her satisfaction almost at once, and then again and again until his powerful body shuddered into completion.

He cursed viciously as he convulsed, his neck corded, his body lifted above hers so that she could watch him. He felt her eyes and then he went actually unconscious for a space of seconds in a blackness of tearing, unbearable pleasure.

She was bending over him, concerned. "Nick?" she whispered worriedly, touching his face with hands that trembled. "Oh, Nick, darling, are you all right?"

His eyes opened. His face was very pale, his body trembling with the strain it had been under. "I tried not to feel like this," he whispered.

"Yes. I know." She bent and smiled as she kissed his eyelids, his mouth. "I love you so much," she choked, her voice full of tears. "I was dying because you didn't want me...!"

He groaned and pulled her down to him, kissing her with feverish emotion. "I love you. I always did. But I was so afraid. You see how it is now, don't you?" he asked bitterly, laughing at his own helplessness. "I let you watch me, because I wanted you to have it all. I'd do anything for you. God, you own me now!"

He seemed shattered by the knowledge that he was helpless when he was with her, as if it made him feel less than a man. She couldn't have that.

She laid her cheek on his chest. "When you're rested," she whispered, "we'll do that again. And this time, you can watch me. Maybe if you see that I'm as totally at your mercy as you just were at mine, you'll realize that what we feel for each other is mutual. There's nothing shameful about it, nothing demeaning." She smiled. "Nick, love is like that. It overpowers, owns. But I can't gloat. I'm only happy that you care so much. I'll never, never make you sorry that you do. I promise."

He began to breathe normally, his moment of weakness slowly passing. He stroked her long hair softly and his body began to relax. "Is it like that for you?" he asked softly. "Do you come close to unconsciousness when I satisfy you?"

"Of course!" She lifted her head and looked down at him curiously. "Didn't you realize?"

"I haven't been able to watch you," he said quietly. "I was too far gone."

She smiled. "Next time, then," she whispered.

His eyes softened. "If I can control myself that long," he said with black humor.

"We've got all our lives," she told him. "All the rest of our lives to feel and share and love and be together. Risk everything, Nick," she whispered. "That's the only way to really love."

"Yes," he replied, and his eyes kindled. "I suppose it is." He searched her face. His lean hands caught her bare waist and lifted her to lie on him. "I've been running. If I let myself care, I knew it would be like it just was. I'd be helpless in my need, in my love, and if I lost you..." He took a deep breath. "Maybe Lucy's death affected me in ways I didn't realize. But I think I'm getting it all back in perspective. There are no guarantees. Only love. And we have that. My God, we have it!" he said fervently.

"Forever and ever," she sighed, and bent to kiss him again.

He pulled the coverlet over them partially and closed his eyes. He was committed now. It didn't feel so bad. In fact, he thought, looking down at Tabby's sleeping face, it felt like heaven. He closed his own eyes and let himself drift. Funny, he thought as he drifted off, that captivity and freedom suddenly felt the same. When he woke up, he'd have to puzzle that out. Right now, he was living a dream and he didn't want it to end a minute too soon. His arms contracted gently around his wife, and he smiled in his sleep.

*   *   *   *   *

SILHOUETTE® *Desire*™

COMING NEXT MONTH

#721 SHIPWRECKED!—Jackie Merritt
Miles Leighton was insufferable, rude, and Lexie Wallis couldn't *stand* him! Then they were stranded on a desert isle, and a bump on the head turned Miles from dreadful to dream boat....

#722 FLIRTING WITH TROUBLE—Cathie Linz
Determined to expose a gambling ring, librarian Nicole Larson was prepared to risk it all. And after one look at sexy undercover detective Chase Ellis, she knew she was flirting with trouble.

#723 PRINCESS McGEE—Maura Seger
Lucas Messina wanted revenge on Lorelei McGee for his uncle's death. Yet when he found she wasn't the ice princess he expected, how could he do anything but fall in love?

#724 AN UNSUITABLE MAN FOR THE JOB—Elizabeth Bevarly
Alexis Marchand thought Ramsey Walker was an arrogant, overgrown adolescent. He thought *she* was a prude. Could a tug-of-war between these two opposites lead to a perfect match?

#725 SOPHIE'S ATTIC—Robin Elliott
Hot on the trail of his ex-partner's murderer, secret agent Tyson McDonald knew he had to protect his friend's daughter, sultry Sophie Clarkson. But who would protect her from *him?*

#726 MIDNIGHT RIDER—Cait London
July's *Man of the Month,* Dan Blaylock, had to keep his hands off Hannah Jordan years ago. But now, the smart-mouthed, stubborn woman needed a rough rider to keep an eye on her....

AVAILABLE NOW—June Grooms:

Take 4 bestselling love stories FREE

Plus get a FREE surprise gift!

Special Limited-time Offer

Mail to Silhouette Reader Service™

In the U.S.	In Canada
3010 Walden Avenue	P.O. Box 609
P.O. Box 1867	Fort Erie, Ontario
Buffalo, N.Y. 14269-1867	L2A 5X3

YES! Please send me 4 free Silhouette Desire® novels and my free surprise gift. Then send me 6 brand-new novels every month, which I will receive months before they appear in bookstores. Bill me at the low price of $2.49* each—a savings of 40¢ apiece off the cover prices. There are no shipping, handling or other hidden costs. I understand that accepting the books and gift places me under no obligation ever to buy any books. I can always return a shipment and cancel at any time. Even if I never buy another book from Silhouette, the 4 free books and the surprise gift are mine to keep forever.

*Offer slightly different in Canada—$2.49 per book plus 69¢ per shipment for delivery. Canadian residents add applicable federal and provincial sales tax. Sales tax applicable in N.Y.

225 BPA ADMA   326 BPA ADMP

Name _____ (PLEASE PRINT) _____

Address _____ Apt. No. _____

City _____ State/Prov. _____ Zip/Postal Code _____

This offer is limited to one order per household and not valid to present Silhouette Desire® subscribers. Terms and prices are subject to change.

DES-92   © 1990 Harlequin Enterprises Limited

SILHOUETTE
Desire
10TH
Anniversary

Celebrate with a FREE classic collection of romance!

In honor of its 10th anniversary, Silhouette Desire has a gift for you! A limited edition, hardcover anthology of three early Silhouette Desire titles, written by three of your favorite authors:

> **DIANA PALMER**—*September Morning*
> **JENNIFER GREENE**—*Body and Soul*
> **LASS SMALL**—*To Meet Again*

This unique collection will not be available in retail stores and is only available through this exclusive offer.

Send your name, address and zip or postal code, along with six proof-of-purchase coupons from any Silhouette Desire published in June, July or August, plus $2.75 for postage and handling (check or money order—please do not send cash) payable to Silhouette Books, to:

In the U.S.	In Canada
Desire 10th Anniversary	Desire 10th Anniversary
Silhouette Books	Silhouette Books
3010 Walden Avenue	P.O. Box 609
P.O. Box 9057	Fort Erie, Ontario
Buffalo, NY 14269-9057	L2A 5X3

(Please allow 4-6 weeks for delivery. Hurry! Quantities are limited. Offer expires September 30, 1992.)

SDANPOP-R

SILHOUETTE DESIRE
10TH ANNIVERSARY
proof-of-purchase

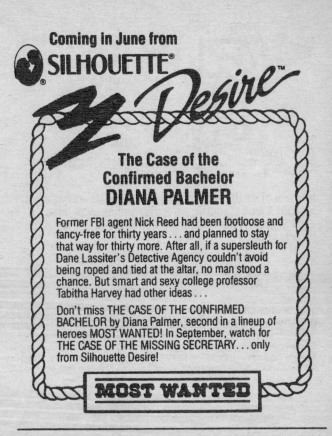